LAST SUNDAY

books by Robert Newton Peck

A DAY NO PIGS WOULD DIE

PATH OF HUNTERS

MILLIE'S BOY

SOUP

FAWN

WILD CAT

SOUP & ME

BEE TREE

HANG FOR TREASON

HAMILTON

RABBITS AND REDCOATS

KING OF KAZOO

TRIG

LAST SUNDAY

LAST SUNDAY

ROBERT NEWTON PECK

Illustrated by Ben Stahl

DOUBLEDAY & COMPANY, INC.
GARDEN CITY, NEW YORK

Library of Congress Cataloging in Publication Data

Peck, Robert Newton.
    Last Sunday.

    SUMMARY: Twelve-year-old mascot Babe helps her
aging friend and pitcher Sober McGinty arrive in time for
the antics at Durkee's Lot when two local teams meet for
the biggest game of the season.
    [1. Baseball—Fiction]   I. Stahl, Ben F.   II. Title.
PZ7.P339Las   [Fic]
ISBN 0-385-12531-3 Trade
        0-385-12532-1 Prebound
Library of Congress Catalog Card Number 76–42381

To Norm
and all the Colonials

LAST SUNDAY

CHAPTER 1

"How is he?"

"Quiet!" hollered Doc. "I can't listen to his heart with you pack of numbskulls asking a lot of tomfool questions. Where'd you people learn to whisper, in a sawmill?" Doc was as deaf as he was blind.

I was on my knees in the dirt, holding Sober's hand. The menfolk and I all did our darnedest to be still while Doc Tussy, with the tubes of his old stethoscope dangling from his ears like a wiggly pair of black worms, leaned and rolled his eyes as he tried to hear Sober McGinty's heartbeat.

"It's his heart," mumbled Kirby Stinnit, which sort of made everybody look at Kirby as if he'd recently announced there was salt in the ocean.

"How'd it happen?"

"Drunk, I suppose, like he usual is on Sunday morning."

"Who found him?"

"They say Marv Higbee found him."

"Where?"

"Over yonder, stretched out in the bin of a wagon. Seems like Marv and his missus was coming out of the Methodist church, no more'n ten minutes ago, and there was Sober McGinty, out cold."

Well, I'd seen Sober a mite misty on Sunday morning before, but not so bad off that he'd vacant his usual seat in the very back row of the Methodist's.

We all stood there looking at Sober McGinty's peaceful face, wanting to ask the one question that cut to the core of the only thing that mattered in this whole town on this one Sunday. I wanted to ask, too; but as I was only twelve years old, I figured some grownup would speak up, and I was right. Somebody finally asked:

"Doc?"

"Yeah?"

"Can he pitch this afternoon?"

"Sure," said Doc, "he can pitch . . . provided he does it lying down at the mound and resting his head on the rubber."

"He ain't dead, is he?"

Doc said, "No, but he's dead drunk. Must of got really tanked up last evening."

Mama had told me not to wander off while she was inside the drugstore getting a copy of the Sunday paper, the *Free Press*. Just about everybody here in

Canby and in the whole world read the *Free Press* on Sunday, whether you lived in Vermont or anywhere else. Well, I really hadn't wandered off. I'd only slipped around the corner when I heard all the ruckus over finding Sober McGinty; and I was just standing there among all the menfolk, when I felt Mama's hand on my shoulder. It was far from gentle. And if anyone could holler out a hush it was my mother:

"Ruth Babson!"

My name (I was thinking as Mama jerked my arm a bit harder than necessary to get my attention) was no worse than a passel of others I've heard. Seeing as I *am* Ruth Babson, I don't guess I'll complain that I can't live with it, even though it wasn't pretty . . . like Shirley Temple or Bobby Breen or Deanna Durbin.

"Just look at your stockings!" she said, whispering like an early kettle.

Nobody, including me, looked at my white stockings. Because with Sober McGinty still on the ground, out cold, there was lots better things to be concerned about, seeing as today was the Four of July. In a matter of a few hours, half of Canby would be at the baseball field, Durkee's Lot, to razz the visiting team from Wiggin. A year ago, almost everybody in Canby had to go to Wiggin as we were the visiting team. But this year, the biggest baseball game of the season was going to be right here in

Canby. You'd have to be crazy to absent today's game. Everybody knew that Sober McGinty was going to pitch for the Canby Catfish.

Half of our town was opposed to baseball on Sunday, but those same folks would be at Durkee's Lot tonight, for the Revival.

My eyes must be playing tricks on me, I thought, on account that Sober never missed his Sunday baseball. Only once, somebody had remembered. Twenty years ago, or maybe even thirty, Sober McGinty had missed a game because he had been courting Gladice Appling at the time. So folks said. The two of them were walking home on a Saturday night, when they took a detour through Lick Donovan's pasture. According to Gladice, Sober had just bent over to pick up a buttercup when he caught a hoof from Lick's mule, Jacqueline.

"Can't I even get a newspaper," Mama asked me in her annoyed voice as she snaked me down the street away from all the excitement, "without your getting clay mud on the knees of your best church stockings? Just look at yourself!"

They had found Sober out cold in Lick's pasture, I was recalling from the legend that had been passed down in Canby from generation to generation. They didn't find Gladice Appling; but for some reason they found a half-empty bottle of Husky Gin, a lump on Sober, and an article of Gladice's clothing.

"Just wait until I get you home," said Mama.

Actually, from what the history of Canby recorded, it wasn't the lump from Lick Donovan's mule that caused Sober to miss the game the next day. The real reason was Charlie Appling (who was engaged to Gladice at the time) who waited in the dugout that Sunday along with a shotgun that folks said would have graded Mount Mansfield.

"How did your stockings get so muddy in just five minutes?"

When my mother went mad over some little thing, she usual said "just" a whole lot, near to every breath. It was just as if what she was so het-up about was the only matter, and she couldn't be bothered with more important issues, like Sober's condition.

"They found McGinty," I said to Mama as we left Main Street and turned up Elm. That's when I smiled to Felix Hoop who drove the only taxicab in Canby. It was a Terraplane, and some said it could go up to forty. Felix never drove it over twenty.

"Hi, Felix," I chirped at him, as he cut back a rosebush that was pulling over his trellis. He was tall and skinny, with a grin that sort of suited Sunday morning.

"Howdy there, Babe!"

"*Mister* Hoop," my mother whispered.

"He told me to call him Felix. Everyone else does."

"Well, no one your age."

"String Pendle does."

"I wouldn't copy anything *he* does."

"You mean like during a spelling test?"

"No, and you know perfectly well . . ."

"Nice morning, Miz Babson."

"Yes, it certainly is." Mama smiled at Felix but didn't stop.

"I bet Babe can't wait for this after."

"Oh, you mean Ruth." Mama sort of glared at me, like she always did whenever somebody called me Babe. She scowls even harder when Papa forgets and calls me Babe. Everybody calls me Babe, because there isn't one single soul in Canby that doubts for one single second that I can throw a slider near as good as Sober McGinty, even though I'm only twelve. Nobody but Sober told me how to throw a slider. Even away before that, it was Sober McGinty who stopped calling me Ruth and started calling me Babe.

I was fixing to stop and give Felix Hoop a report on Sober's sorry state of health, even though temporary, but I already felt the push Mama's hand gave my shoulder. As if to say that she had no intention whatever of pausing to chat, and that she wanted to hurry home in order to put the chicken in the oven. One thing to be thankful for, at least it was chicken. Pork takes longer.

"So long, Babe!"

"Good-bye, Mister Hoop."

"See ya at the ball park!" he yelled.

"You betcha!" I hollered back.

Mama *just* sighed. "Just once," she said, as we continued down Elm Street, "I would like to have *one* Sunday dinner, just one, that isn't rushed through because people have to see some [she wanted to say *damn*] . . . baseball game."

"Today's kind of a special game."

"According to you," said Mama, "every game is. When I was a girl, people had some respect for the Sabbath. We weren't allowed to play baseball on Sunday. There was a local ordinance against it."

"You mean baseball was against the *law?*"

"On Sunday, yes."

"It's the only day to play," I said.

"That's not true."

"But the men work their jobs the other six days."

Mama sighed as we walked along. "Yes, I know they do. Hard workers, most of them, and they all deserve to have a little fun."

"There's talk around town," I said, "of people quitting early on Saturday, closing up the stores, and having the game then."

"Who said that?"

"Gladice Appling."

Mama said nothing. She was always silent as sin whenever I mentioned Gladice Appling's name. They'd gone to school together, back in olden times when Papa and Mama and Gladice and Sober and all the rest of the old people were kids. But he wasn't called Sober in those days.

His righteous name was Dan McGinty.

Some of the fans in Durkee's Lot started to call him Diz, on account he pitched so doggone good. You know, after Dizzy Dean who pitched for the Cards. But the Diz never stuck. I don't guess Sober would go by any other handle, seeing that was the way we hoped to find him on Sunday morning.

If the Sunday baseball game did get moved up to Saturday, maybe Canby would be better fixed to win the county pennant. Plenty of folks in town said that Sober might not throw so wild as he worked the first inning if he did his pitching *before* Saturday night, instead of after.

"That's what Gladice Appling said," I told Mama again. As we walked down the shady side of Elm Street, there lay a little tin can on the walkway, and I kicked it. The can went clanking along the white pickets of Miss Hewlitt's fence, banged up against a fireplug, and finally come to rest.

"Gladice Appling says more than her prayers."

"Most folks do," I agreed.

"Ruth, don't be sassy."

"I'm sorry, Mama. You're one heck of a peachy mom and I wouldn't sass you, or Papa. Not for anything."

"Sometimes you come very close."

"I know. Not on purpose. To tell you the straight

of it, I sure wouldn't want to do anything *today* to get you so riled up that you'd send me up to my room until supper." I smiled at her.

"Because of that *game,* I suppose." She smiled back.

"Today it's Wiggin."

"Will we win? Not that I care one bit, and I don't even know why I'm asking, but does Canby have a chance?"

"No," I said, "not without McGinty."

CHAPTER 2

Honk!

Even before Mama and I turned the corner off Elm and started along Jay Street, I heard Aunt Hobart's horn. Only one squeeze of the bulb made me almost forget worrying about Sober McGinty.

Running ahead, in spite of its being Sunday morning when hurrying was tantamount to damnation, I never stopped running until I could frog over the Harrison's privet hedge and there, parked in our driveway, was one beauty of a pea-green Model-A Ford.

"Aunt Hobart!"

There she was, one of the tallest and leanest creatures that Nature ever had the humor to dream up. Six feet tall, she told me once, even though I had been warned by Mama never to ask. She'd sort of hinted that Aunt Hobart never got wed because of her height, but that couldn't be. Besides, you'd have to look a while before finding a husband who'd deserve Aunt Hobart for a wife. She held out her hands and yelled to me.

"Babe!"

Her long arms were open, and when I got to her, around me they went. We hugged like she was leaving.

"Wow, am I glad to see you, Aunt Hobart!"

"No gladder than I am to see you." One more hug and then she ordered me to stand up straight and to allow her a good look at me. A slight twitch of her mouth told me that she spied the mud patched on the knees of my white stockings, and her smile that followed said that a few dabs of mud on me was to be expected.

"My, how you've grown since last summer."

She had on her lavender dress; and, like always, a large white hanky with lace on all four sides was anchored to her dress-front by an amethyst brooch. The hanky was sort of floppy like a flower. That was when I almost said I hoped I'd be as tall as she was because height sure whips a pitch, but I kept silent. There was no way I'd ever want to hurt Aunt Hobart's feelings. Sure wouldn't.

Aunt Hobart waved to Mama who was walking our way; but while she smiled at my mother (and without moving her lips), she said: "Quick now, Babe, what time's the game?"

"Two o'clock," I said, not moving mine.

"Good."

"If I know Mama," I said out of the side of my mouth, "two o'clock will be recess for the roast."

"Keep calm," said Aunt Hobart. "I have a plan, just in case Sunday dinner tastes a bit tardy. I'll just tell your mom that you and I've got work to do for the Revival tonight. Hush for now."

"Well," said Mama as the two ladies kissed each other's cheek, "we weren't expecting you until later this afternoon, Hobart. You certainly made good time."

Using the flat of her hand, Aunt Hobart presented a pair of tinny pats to a pea-green fender. "Lizzie was anxious as I was to visit you folks. You're looking well, Mildred."

"So are you. Things must be fine up in Ewington."

"Same as always. Where's Alf?"

"Probably," sighed Mama, "where he always is."

"Under his Hudson."

"Where else?"

"My valise is in the rumble."

"Alf will fetch it. He's around back."

The long legs of Alfred T. Babson, my father, protruded out from under our Hudson. Beneath our car he logged many a summer hour, tinkering on this and touching up that, whanging and banging, swearing and tearing. The Hudson never did, according to Papa, run right. Yet our machine managed to endure his constant repair and I give credit to the Hudson people that it ran as well as it did. He had converted it, gasket-by-geegaw, into one of Vermont's mechanical marvels. He had replaced so many parts which *he* found to be substandard that very little of the original Hudson limped into our garage at sundown. In fact, in all fairness, we couldn't really claim it was still a Hudson.

Our car was a Babson.

My father was under the car. Summer upon summer, the only spots on Papa's entirety that got touched by sunlight were the near hairless expanses of his shins, between where the cuffs of his pants edged up and where his white work socks sagged down. Only from belt to toe was visible; the remainder of Alfred T. Babson was under the machine. His legs stretched out straight as he was one of the few folks in the county who was taller than Aunt Hobart, his sister.

We heard a clank, a mash, and an oath. Three sounds in familiar order that our backyard atmosphere had grown accustomed to with each passing season of repair.

"Hit your thumb, Alf?"

"Dang it. That you, Hobart?"

"It isn't Mae West."

Very little could have enticed my father out from under his car on a Sunday. Aunt Hobart did. Out he crawled and up he stood, giving her a hearty kiss on the cheek, allowing her to leave a ruby swatch on his face, while depositing on hers a healthy black smear of what should have been drained from a crankcase.

"Did I get oil on ya? Hope so," he grinned.

"No matter," said Aunt Hobart. "I'll just wipe it off on the next guy."

We all laughed. Papa ragged the motor oil off his hands in order to tote Aunt Hobart's valise up to the guest room. Every summer she stayed over one night and then packed off the following morning, as she professed she didn't want to overstay her welcome. Mama slipped her best apron (pink gingham checkerboard with frills and a double pocket) over her head to protect her church dress and prepared the chicken for cookery.

Papa returned to torment the car.

I helped set the table. And then Aunt Hobart and I took ourselves a Sunday stroll out in the backyard until we got to the shade trees. While I rode the swing, Aunt Hobart pushed me. Then we sat on a stump to talk about one of our very favorite subjects . . . baseball.

"How's the arm, Babe?"

"Strikes all the way," I said.

"Your curve breaking?"

"Down and away . . . if I'm hot."

"Hooks are tricky," said Aunt Hobart.

"Yeah, if you have to chuck a dry ball."

"Using a spitter, are you?"

"If I get behind the count. A little spit gives me a tighter grip so the snap on the release is a mite sharper."

"No problems on your fast ball?"

"Steams right in if my control's on. Actually it's the floater that's giving me grief. Either that or the knuckler."

"How so?"

"They're stealing second on my slow stuff."

"Don't let them do that, Babe."

"My move to first isn't so red hot, and when I hurry the pick-off, sometimes the ball goes wild."

Aunt Hobart walked up and down, hands behind her back, slightly stooped and thinking. "How big a lead are the runners taking?"

"Depends."

"On what?"

"Well," I said, "whether the field's wet or dry."

"That makes sense."

"If the base paths are dry, the runner will stretch his lead and also get a quicker break toward second. Mud shortens 'em up."

Aunt Hobart chewed a blade of grass. Placing it between her thumbs, she took a deep breath to blow on it, and really made it trumpet.

"And I don't guess my being a girl helps matters much."

"You the only girl?" asked my aunt.

"Not always; sometimes Cleo McKelvie plays when her ma doesn't know about it. Cleo's mother doesn't favor baseball for girls a whole lot." Like mine, I was thinking.

"Same thing when I was a girl. Enough on history. Who's your first baseman?"

"String Pendle."

"Is he mean?"

"Like sin."

"Best you play possum on the first throw and gamble on the second."

"How?" I asked her.

Underneath the swing was a bare patch of dry dirt where you scuffed your feet so much that the grass never grew. On her knees, Aunt Hobart drew a diamond in the dust, no more than a yard from home to first.

"Looky," she said. "Let your runner ease off on his first lead. Make a soft throw to first, faking a bigger motion, to make him think that's your best move. Got it?"

"I think so."

She moved an acorn an inch. "Now your *second* throw to first is when you'll get him. You . . . or what was that gink's name?"

"String Pendle."

"Is he stringy and strong?"

"Sure is."

"Good. After your first throw, the runner will feel cocky enough to stretch his lead off the sack. Throw fast, so he can't make it back standing up. He'll have to dive back to the bag on his belly. Here, I'll show you."

"Okay," I said, as we moved over on the grass.

"I'm playing first base. I'm String and you're the runner, Babe. Okay, take your lead toward second. Ease off, that's it, and dance a little. You're cocky now, having seen that pitcher's slow move to first."

"Now what?"

"Ever see slow motion at the picture show?"

"Lots of times."

"Then that's how we'll do it. You're the runner. My pocketbook is the sack. I'm old String. Here comes the pitcher's throw, the hard one that's really steaming. Slowly now, come back to the bag on your belly. Careful and don't grass-stain your dress or heck won't have it. Reach for the base with your right hand, to guard your face. Got it? Stop!"

I stopped, my stomach frozen to the lawn, my hand stretching beneath Aunt Hobart to her pocketbook behind her right shoe, which said Red Cross inside the heel.

"Aim your throw high enough to let your friend String make the tag *hard*. Harder than Hades. More of a punch than a tag. As you lie there, Mr. Runner, see how exposed your neck is? And your ear? If the tag is early, fine and dandy. He's out. *But* even if the tag is late, String will give your would-be base stealer one whale of a whack. Bury the ball right in his ear."

"I get it. So on the third lead, he'll hug close enough to get back standing up."

"Right you are."

"Thanks a lot, Aunt Hobart."

"Nothing to it. That runner of yours now can't be thinking about second base as much as the lump on his neck. You'll cut his lead in half, and he won't start off so rabbit quick."

It was Aunt Hobart's turn in the swing. I pushed her.

CHAPTER 3

"My," said Aunt Hobart, "that's some chicken."

"Best you ever roasted," said Papa, helping himself to more biscuits and gravy.

"That goes double for me," I said. "I'm full up."

My mother beamed the smile of a contented cook who was determined to stuff her tablemates as fully as she had stuffed the fowl. Mama herself was a bit on the plump side, yet it never seemed to slow down her knife and fork.

"Another slice of white meat, Hobart?"

"Mercy me no. Not that it wasn't first rate, Mildred, because it certainly was."

"Sure was, Mama." I could see how my mother wanted to spoon out another portion to people so she herself could wolf down a second helping and not appear too piggy.

"Ruth," said my mother to me, "I *do* wish you'd have yourself another helping. That girl," she turned to my aunt, "is little more than skin and bone. Not an ounce of flesh on her."

"Same way when I was twelve," said Papa.

Our parlor clock struck one o'clock, tightening the muscles of my stomach; and for some reason, my hands pushed downward on the edges of my chair seat as though I was preparing to leave the table.

"Ruth Babson," my mother said, "not one word about the Canby Catfish or Durkee's Lot until dinner is over. We are not going to run this house around some baseball game from June until Labor Day."

"Sorry," I said, forcing my body to ease down.

"Tonight's the Revival," said Aunt Hobart, "which is my main reason for coming to Canby, other than to see you folks, of course. I'm quite anxious to hear the Reverend Buddy Dee."

"So am I," said Mama.

One o'clock, I was thinking, and here I sit, still in my church dress. Up in my bedroom closet hung the costume I really hankered to be inside. However, had I worn a baseball uniform to the Sunday dinner table, such an action could have wiped out all my chances of getting to Durkee's Lot by warm-up, or watching the Warriors arrive from Wiggin in their big yellow bus.

I was also thinking about Sober McGinty.

Years back, when I was just a kid, I always used to dream about being a grown-up lady, and marrying Sober. I'd be Mrs. Dan McGinty. Never did I contemplate getting myself wed to anyone but. As I grew a little older, Sober McGinty became a whole lot older, and grayer, which sort of convinced me

that marrying Sober would be almost as much fun as
living all over again with Papa. How, I suddenly
asked my own thoughts, would it be to spend every
Sunday seeing little more than my husband's legs
protruding out from under a motorcar? A dead stork.

No, I don't guess I'd wed Sober.

Who then? Well, surely not String Pendle. Or not
any other boy I went to school with. But especially
not String Pendle. Sometimes I would close my eyes
at night and pretend I was married, living in my
own house; not here in Canby but in some other
place, real far off. Then the dream world would
come crashing to an end whenever I would take an
imaginary saunter out into my own backyard and
suddenly see another Hudson, with String's long legs
poking out from under the running board.

I knew they were String's legs. Which made me
Mrs. Jude Pendle for the rest of my born days.

My mother spent much of her time hollering
sweetly out the back door: "Alf! Supper's on."
Which only on the second or third try managed to
pry him out from below the muffler. Once in the
dream I called out back: "Jude! Supper's on!" And
it sure sounded spooky. Woke me up out of a sound
sleep and for most of an hour I lay awake, staring at
my bedroom ceiling where the paint was peeling, and
seeing String Pendle's legs.

Time was ticking on.

We'd have pie to eat, and then Mama would be

sitting over a hot cup of tea as though it was a real pleasure for Papa (who wanted to get back under the Hudson) and me (who wanted to rush off to Durkee's Lot) to see her sip it. Yet it was selfish, I was thinking, to expect Mama to turn out a nifty meal and then watch folks gobble it down on the run to get somewheres else. Guess there's two sides to it, like to most things. A baseball game wouldn't be much unless there were two sides. Canby against Wiggin. The Catfish are playing the Warriors in less than an hour, and Mama will sip tea like nothing's going on.

"Don't guess I'll have dessert," I said.

My mother glared at me, reading my thoughts, defying me with one of her stern glances, as though to warn me that if I as much as mentioned baseball, I would spend the afternoon confined to my room and Bible reading.

We ate apple pie laced with cinnamon and nutmeg which was really top of the order.

Papa and Hobart and I demolished our pie in about three hearty bites, no more than four. Mama, just to be contrary, took a speck at a time on her fork, so small that I was concerned it might fall between the tines. In school, Miss Logan told us all how important it was to chew each mouthful fifty times, for the sake of proper digestion. All I could think of was how perfect my mother's digestion was that Sunday.

"Babe," said Aunt Hobart, "it's time. If I'm to help set up for the Revival this evening, I suppose I'd best go to take a look at this Durkee location."

Mama's eyes widened. Papa's hands fidgeted with his napkin as though he longed to fondle a lug wrench.

"I surrender," sighed Mama, shoving her last bite of apple pie (a good hunk) into her mouth, gulping it down along with a quick wash of tea that drained her cup. She was aping all of us doggone well, and Mama's antics made me snicker.

"We'll help do the dishes," said Aunt Hobart, "won't we, Babe?"

"Please," said Mama, raising her hands in protest as if to ward off assistance. "Every cup and saucer would be thrown around the kitchen table like a double play, whatever that is. Just *go,* everybody. I'll clean up in leisure, read the *Free Press,* and perhaps take a nap out in the hammock. I can't abide another moment on the edge of our chairs. Mercy, it's like you're all crouching at a starting line, waiting for a gun to go off."

"Let's go, Babe!" said Aunt Hobart.

In a minute flat, I skinned out of my church dress and into my baseball uniform and purple cap. On the back of the shirt was my number, a big O, and across my chest in purple letters was CANBY. The uniform was originally white, now gray, with pinstripes down through the shirt and pants, just like the New York Yankees. Most folks in town rooted for two teams and two teams only, the Boston Red Sox and the Canby Catfish. There were no Yankee fans in town. Supporting the Yanks would have made one nearly as unpopular as cheering the Wiggin Warriors on the Four of July.

"What time is it, Aunt Hobart?" I asked her as the two of us bolted across our front lawn in the direction of the pea-green Model-A. I tossed my baseball glove into the car.

"Near to half-past one, so best we shake a leg."

Between coaxing and threats from Aunt Hobart, Lizzie's engine started up, sputtered, and then died in silence. Carrying his tool kit, Papa rushed around the corner of the house just as my aunt had dismounted from behind the wheel and had lifted up the folding hood flap.

"Maybe I'll take a look at her," offered Papa, a menacing wrench already in hand.

Turning about like a cornered cobra, Aunt Hobart placed her back to her coupe and confronted my father. "Alf Babson, don't you get any notions about doctoring up my Lizzie." She looked like Barbara Frietchie defending the flag.

"Want to borrow the Hudson?"

"And leave poor Lizzie here with you to tinker on?" said Aunt Hobart, her jaw thrust slightly forward in a posture of defiance. "Oh no, Alf. Handing you a hammer is like giving whiskey to a drunk."

"I wouldn't touch your old car and you know it," said Papa. He looked a mite miffed.

A minute later, as my father watched in disappointment, the Model-A finally decided to crank herself up and be co-operative. As Lizzie's motor went put-put-put, Papa yelled to Hobart: "I might give her a tune-up when you get back."

"Over my dead body and fender," shouted Aunt Hobart.

Backing carefully out of our driveway, Aunt Hobart gripped the wheel with a headlock, and we chugged merrily down Jay Street in the direction of Durkee's Lot.

"Hold it!" I said.

"Babe, we'll miss the warm-up."

"So will Sober."

"He's your pitcher, isn't he?"

"He sure is."

"Well, what about him?"

"Just a hunch. His shack's uproad about a mile out of town."

"A *mile?*"

"Maybe not quite. Church people took him home this morning, the way I got it figured, and maybe just dumped him and forgot about the game."

"What's the matter with Sober?"

"He got drunk last night."

"Doesn't he always?"

"Sure, but he missed church," I said.

"So did I and I'm still kicking. Which way?"

"Straight ahead"—I pointed—"where Jay Street turns into Jay Road."

"We're off. Hang onto your cap."

"I heard about the Revival tonight. We had one here in Canby a few summers back. Mama and Papa went. Guess I was too little. Are they fun?"

"They can be. Although *fun* may be not quite the word to describe it," said Aunt Hobart. "Lots of folks get Saved."

"You mean getting Saved can sort of change your whole life?"

"It honest can. I mean it, Babe. Not that I'm nuts about religion. But on the other hand, I'm not exactly against it."

"Are you a Methodist, like us?"

"No, I'm a Baptist. And I mean it when I say this, Babe. A good Saving never hurt anybody. Never let it be said that Hobart Babson was on the side of the devil."

A fork in the dirt road made her ask, "Which way?"

"To the left."

"You come up here often?"

"Only a few times. Just to sort of look in on Sober and get him to Durkee's Lot on time. We're proud of him, you know."

"I know. And I'm proud of you. Tickled pink when Alf called up on the contraption to tell me that his Babe was going to be mascot for the Catfish this season."

"I'm only the bat boy."

"Don't you mean bat *girl?*"

"Guess I do. Number Zero."

"For how many home games have you been the mascot?"

"Today'll make three."

Lizzie took a puddle or a rut that rattled her more than a mite. "Some road," said Aunt Hobart. "What did all your pals say when a *gal* was chosen?"

"Not too much. Mama fretted a bit, on appearances, as she doesn't want me to grow up to be a hussy. And a few of the guys said some rotten stuff."

"Babe," said Aunt Hobart, "there will always be people to throw things your way. Some of them can hurt worse than a baseball. But if you're a lady, as I know you'll be one day, all the beanballs in Vermont will bounce off."

"Will they?" I asked her.

"Sure enough will."

"And will I lose my freckles?"

She laughed. "I lost mine. But now I have something a lot better than freckles."

"Like what?"

"You."

CHAPTER 4

"Sober!"

At first I thought I was yelling to an empty gray shanty, as we heard not as much as a peep from inside. We climbed out of the Model-A and knocked on the unpainted door. The wood was rough sawed and unsoftened by weather.

"Dan McGinty!" I yelled out.

"Never knew his name was Dan," said Aunt Hobart.

"I don't guess most folks do."

"You prefer Dan or Sober?"

"Dan," I said.

From inside came a moan, so we pushed open the door. Sure enough, there was McGinty, stretched out on his cot and still in his Saturday-night clothes. Except that his shoes were off. I saw one shoe but not its mate. The place was dark, a coffee pot lay on its side under the small potbelly stove. A smell of stale laundry haunted the place, so I left the door open. The flies were already inside, with three on Dan's

face. Sober looked at both Aunt Hobart and me, from one to the other, not saying a word. His eyes were baby beets.

"Howdy," he grinned. "Hi ya, Babe."

"*He's* your pitcher," asked Aunt Hobart.

"Sure." I tried to make myself chuckle as if what happens to Sober on Saturday night was a town joke. Like watching him almost fall over in the pew on Sunday morning at the Methodist church was a real circus. It wasn't funny to me.

"Who . . . who's your friend, Babe?"

"My aunt. Miss Hobart Babson, may I present Mr. Dan McGinty."

"Nice to meet you, Mr. McGinty."

"S'pleasure."

"How come you're not suited up yet?" The words sort of caught in my throat and came out as shaky as I knew Dan would be if we ever got him up on his feet, which looked unlikely.

"What's today?"

"Sunday, the Four of July."

"Yikers! I gotta pitch."

"Sure do."

"Where . . . where's my uniform?"

Aunt Hobart and I turned Sober McGinty's shack near to upside down. All his clothes hung on pegs. One by one, we took down an overcoat, slicker, poncho, buffalo-plaid hunting jacket, and an old gray sweater. The wool was damp and musty, even though it was summer. On the floor, my foot kicked over an empty gin bottle. Carrying it to the door, I flung it off into the trees, end over end, wanting it to smash to bits as though its breaking could mend up a broken friend.

"Got the time?" he asked. His mouth hung open. On his chin, the gray stubble peeked through his wrinkled face as though to find out if it was sunup.

"Quarter of two," I said in a guess.

With trembling hands holding his temples, he swung his legs down off the squeaking cot and to the rugless wide boards of a floor that had never known varnish, and seldom a broom or mop. There was a hole in the red toe of his gray work sock, allowing his big toenail to moon up at me.

"Babe," he said, "my uniform . . ."

"I found it," said Aunt Hobart, "if this wad is what the man's looking for." She pulled it out from under the foot of his cot. It was in sorry shape.

"Make some coffee," I said.

"Won't help," said Aunt Hobart. "Black coffee to bring people around from a bout with John Barleycorn is an old wives' tale. Only one thing sweats out a bender."

"What's that?"

"Time."

"We don't have much of that," I said. "We have to help to get him dressed, Aunt Hobart."

For a moment, the expression on her face indicated that the idea of redressing our friend McGinty was hardly a proper hobby for my spinster aunt to occupy on a Sunday afternoon.

"Why not," she finally agreed.

Carefully I undid the buttons down the front of his white shirt, while Aunt Hobart pulled off his trousers.

His body looked as rumpled as his clothes. His legs were long and white, shiny and skinny, without any hair. A vein below his knee was large and blue, glowering at me. An inky eye. His underwear were soiled and stained, causing me to close one eye in an attempt to allow Dan McGinty at least half the modesty he deserved. Over his purple jersey, we jerked on his mussy uniform shirt and pants. Number 7.

We found only one long purple sock. Sober's other leg would have to go half bare. Finding his cleats behind the woodbox, I slipped one on one foot while my aunt fitted the other.

"Can you stand?" I asked him, carrying his warm-up jacket.

"Sure."

He stood up. I will never know how. His breath was garbage gas. He even burped a long blast to make sure my nose got a sample of the swill that Saturday night in Canby had served him. My eyes swept around the mess inside his shack in one more quick search for his other purple baseball sock. For some reason I wanted to hide as much of Dan McGinty as I could from the public eye.

"Best we hurry," said Aunt Hobart.

With our pitcher between us, one of his arms around my aunt and the other dangling across my shoulders, we stumbled out into the July sunlight. Sober shut his eyes real tight, yet continued to fumble forward, so we somehow got to the pea-green Model-A Ford. My aunt sat behind the wheel, Sober in the middle, with me on the right so Number 7 wouldn't fall out into the dust of Jay Road.

"Hang on, folks," said Aunt Hobart.

From Sober's shack to Durkee's Lot was all down-hill, so Lizzie covered the ground almost as if she was touching it. Half the time, due to the bumps and our speed which was darn close to thirty, we were up in the Vermont air a good ten inches.

We made it!

Canby's Silver-Cornet Band was attempting a final chorus of "Our Director" as Lizzie wheezed into a parking spot beyond the foul line to the right of first base. The hot-dog stand was open, doing a booming business in half-cooked meat and stale buns, disguised in mustard and relish and ketchup, much of which already appeared on the shirts and blouses of several fans. Fred Rogers sold his big bouquet of colored balloons.

"Field looks good," said Aunt Hobart as she

yanked back the parking brake with a series of long ratchety clicks.

"Ben Sturgis drags it on Saturday, to smooth it up," I said. "Then if he can keep us kids off it, the diamond looks pretty prosperous by Sunday."

Ben had put down white lines from home to the foul poles, left and right. I'd help him do it once in a while. He puts powder-chalk inside a little wheel. Then stretches a twine from home plate to push the wheel atop of. When you take the twine in afterward, your hands get all white and dry.

"What's the argument?" asked Aunt Hobart.

Sol Jessup and Ally Hume each had hold of a white strap, engaged in a tug of war. Between them was second base, and it became apparent that their dispute was where the second sack ought to be anchored. Sol pointed at first, squinting one eye, while Ally sighted on third. Finally they agreed on where second base would find its home, pounding in the two eye-spikes that would peg down the straps.

"Come on," said Aunt Hobart, "and let's get this aging athlete over to the dugout."

"Maybe we ought to drive him over."

"Nope. The walk'll do him good."

"Easy now, Dan," I said.

As the Canby Catfish were in uniform, purple socks and purple caps flashing in the sunshine, and out on the field warming up with two or three pepper games, only a few nearby onlookers paid the

three of us too much mind. I was just as well pleased
at that, as I didn't cotton to have Dan McGinty be
the center of attention, not when he could barely
walk.

"Hey there, Sober!" a few folks said.

"How's he doing, Babe?"

"Fine," I said. "Good as new."

"Sober can't throw unless he's hung over."

"Wring him out. Play ball."

As the three of us walked slowly toward the dugout of the Canby Catfish, I noticed that the Warriors weren't here yet, causing me to wonder why
they were late. Wiggin was only twenty miles away if
you take the old road over Green Mountain.

"I'll make it," grunted Sober.

"You always do, Dan," I said.

His hand rested on my shoulder, and so I put my
cheek down on his knuckles, just to feel his hand on
my face and to let Dan know that I was his pal, no
matter what. Looking down at me as I looked up at
him, he smiled.

"Thanks, Babe."

"Aw forget it."

"Ya look good in your uniform, Ruth Babe."

"So do you, Dan. Like always."

"Hey! Where's my glove?"

"Doggone," I said to Aunt Hobart. "We forgot his
lucky glove. He can't pitch without it."

"Does he throw with it?"

"Of course not. Was it back at his place?"

"Didn't see it," said Aunt Hobart, "but we surely saw everything else."

We got to the ground-level dugout and sat Sober down on the bench, in the shade, where he could sort of collect his wits. Hawg Hogarth was sitting there all alone, all three hundred pounds of him, dressed in his manager's uniform and checking the batting order on the score sheet in his clipboard.

"About time." Hawg looked up without a smile.

"Here he is," I said. "And this is my aunt. She's visiting us from Ewington."

"How do, ma'am, and many thanks."

"How do you do."

"Dan's got to warm up," I said.

"I forgot my glove," laughed Sober, and he near to fell off the bench and into the dust. There was a bare spot in front of both dugouts where the grass didn't grow. On its side, the big yellow-canvas bat bag lay, loaded with our yard-long artillery that would havoc Wiggin pitching.

Aunt Hobart found a seat behind our home-team dugout, right next to Kirby Stinnet, who offered her a handful of popcorn. Their conversation was lost to me as I performed my mascot duties, emptying the bat bag, lining up the brown or pale yellow bats in a neat fan, handles back toward Hawg and me. Our big manager didn't seem too distressed at our pitcher's condition, as he'd seen Sober McGinty in

sorry shape on many a Sunday. Yet the Canby
Catfish always seemed to win more games than we
lost.

"I'll get him a glove," I said.

Running over to Lizzie, I found my own baseball
glove, and brought it back to the dugout, handing it
to Dan.

"Here," I said, flipping it to him.

He dropped it.

"Ya fixing to warm up?" The voice was familiar,
that of Will Farnum, our catcher. He already had on
his purple shinguards, mitt under his left arm. The
chest protector and mask hung on a peg in our
dugout. His purple cap was on backward.

"Sure," said Sober.

Right then came an explosion of boos and car
honks and razzing. The big yellow bus from Wiggin
had arrived.

CHAPTER 5

"Here comes Wiggin!"

Into Durkee's Lot rolled the big yellow bus, its loud claxon horns bugling a taunting challenge, black lettering along the roofline that read WIGGIN CENTRAL SCHOOL. Beneath the row of windows that framed the grinning faces under red caps, a hand-painted banner was stretched along the bus's flank which proclaimed the day's occupants to be none other than the Wiggin Warriors. Behind the yellow bus, a line of dust-covered cars, numbering a score or better, honked their horns to announce that they had also made it over the mountain from Wiggin.

Will Farnum gently tossed an almost-new white baseball to Sober McGinty. I'll never know how, but he somehow caught it, to cup in his right hand as though his fingers were made to wrap around two hunks of hourglass horsehide stitched together with a headless and tailless worm of black thread.

"It's old Joe," somebody yelled and pointed at the school bus from Wiggin.

Whether true or not, rumor persisted that near a tenth of the town of Wiggin bore the family name of Gitbo. Some said it was a French name, away back, and others insisted its origin was Huron Indian. Half of the team from Wiggin was named Gitbo. We all watched as the end of the red-capped and red-socked Warriors poured from the yellow bus. Several of them had dark complexions. The last and the darkest to dismount brought a wail of boos and catcalls from Canby throats. It was the old man himself, Injun Joe Gitbo, the patriarch of the tribe as well as the manager of the Wiggin Warriors.

Stooped and white of hair, he seemed almost too ancient to last out the day. Yet quickly he waved to the jeering crowd, smiling as though he was their returning hero. He wore no uniform. Hawg suited up like any other Catfish, but not old Joe Gitbo. His feet wore mocs, browner than molasses with age, and on his bandy legs what appeared to be deerskin trousers, and a red-and-black checkerboard shirt. His white hair was pulled straight back from his buckeye face, braided into one straight gray rope. On his head was a red baseball cap, which his finger came up to touch, as a courtesy to the hostile crowd that razzed him.

Hawg Hogarth waddled his three hundred pounds of bulk over to where old Joe Gitbo stood and held out a friendly right. They shook hands. Hawg wore a 13 on his big back.

"Play ball!" a voice yelled. It came from behind our dugout and sounded like Lick Donovan.

Sober threw some warm-up pitches.

Listening, I could tell by the thud of the ball into Will Farnum's mitt that Sober didn't have much stuff. Will Farnum wouldn't be needing the sponge in his mitt on this Sunday. Dan threw his hook but it didn't break, and when Will fired it back from his crouch, McGinty fumbled it in my glove.

One of the Warriors, number 8, ran over to whisper something in Joe Gitbo's ear, prompting several of the more adamant Canby rooters to yell out the familiar razz that we had used to rile the Gitbo players ever since Papa took me to my first ball game here in Durkee's Lot:

"What'll I do now, Pa?"

In a way, the hooted question was a jeer, a jab to confound and confuse the Wiggin team; and then again, it was respect of a sort. Nobody, I was told by Dan McGinty one day when we were both working on throwing our sinkers, knew more about baseball than Injun Joe Gitbo.

"What'll I do now, Pa?" echoed another local wit from Canby. It was our war cry against Wiggin.

"Play ball!" another voice pleaded, no doubt from a farmer who had to be back home in his barn by chore time; in Vermont, milking got favored over fun.

Frank Murphy, the smallest man on the field, ap-

peared in his pink face and black suit. Murph um-
pired every home game, which gave our home team
(as always) a more than modest chance of victory.
Murph's partisan eye allowed no such phenomenon as
a close play at the plate. A sliding Catfish would be
called "Safe!" by Murph if he was tagged better
than halfway between third and home.

Murph got paid a dollar a game for officiating,
the dollar extracted from the Catfish Fund, money
that originated from the hot-dog stand that had to
kickback part of its Sunday take to support the ball
club. Some folks said that Riley Shattuck, who cooked
the ten-cent hot dogs and passed out the lukewarm
soda pop, also had established what was locally
known as the Riley Shattuck Fund. One time when
Riley drove down the street behind the wheel of a
new DeSoto, somebody yelled out:

"Hey! There goes our dugout!"

Canby took the field, as Murph bent over to dust
home plate with the tiny whiskbroom that he kept in a
hip pocket of his black trousers.

"Play ball!" he officially yelled.

Sober, wearing my glove out on the mound, threw
one more warm-upper, and Will Farnum's practice
peg rifled past Sober's ear to Vernal Klaus who
waited at second. In our near-to-empty dugout, I sat
next to Hawg. His clipboard informed me that the
first batter that McGinty would face would be Hank

Gitbo, their third sacker. Behind the plate, both Will and Murph pulled the masks over their faces. Hank tapped sand off his left heel for a pair of whacks and dug his cleats into the batter's box. I wondered if he was old Joe Gitbo's son, or grandson, or great-grandson. Hank Gitbo crowded the plate, leaning in with a low stance, and Sober had told me once that Hank was a no-hit big-glove thirder who was tough to pitch to. Hank never went for a bad ball. You had to come to him with stuff in (or *near,* if Murph was umpiring) the strike zone—letters to knees.

"Brush him back," whispered Hawg, hoping that Sober would throw inside and cozy, to allow his second pitch curve some working room.

Sober McGinty threw his fast ball which tailed away high. Will's mitt jumped up and pulled it in. Ball one. Ball two on a hook that just didn't break, even though it crowded Hank's batting posture an inch or so. Would he take two and nothing? He did, as Sober's slider came in on a bat handle that had no notion of a healthy cut. I could see the ball-three grin on Hank Gitbo's coppery face; he was lucky that he wasn't swinging on the slider, or else he'd been holding a bundle of splinters.

Hank took for strike one. Every throat in Durkee's Lot yelled like we were on fire. From the corner of my eye I could see the Wiggin dugout, and had seen old Joe Gitbo cross his legs. He uncrossed them, in-

dicating that Hank perhaps could swing away on the fifth pitch. Hey, I swiped a sign!

Ball four!

A groan came from Canby hearts as Hank tossed his bat to the bat boy (probably another young Gitbo) and trotted smoothly down the white line of fresh chalk toward where rangy Gil Haskin, our Catfish first baseman, awaited him. Just by watching Hank Gitbo trot, I knew he was a sack hound. That easy lope to first promised a second and even third gear of speed.

Sober had said that once to me about the Warriors one day when he was showing me how a pick-off play could work. "Wiggin don't often get good wood on the ball, but they can beat you every time on the base path."

Almost as though Hawg knew what I was remembering, he suddenly spoke up. "Yeah, that's how they beat us last year."

"How?" I asked.

"Not on hits. They'd wangle a run on a walk, a steal, a bunt, and a sacrifice fly. Not on hits, Babe."

"Who's up next?"

"Jerry Keen."

"What's he play?"

"Short."

"Can he hit?"

"Nope. But he's long on patience. You'll see."

Down at first, Gil was playing over the bag, trying

to hold Hank on without a big lead toward second. Sober bluffed a quick throw before his foot took the rubber, took a half-stretch with a look over his left shoulder and delivered toward home. Hank didn't go. As the hook hit Will Farnum's mitt, ball one, I checked the Wiggin dugout with my eyes glued on Joe. Up came the brown hand to tug at the red visor of his baseball cap. Steal?

There was no way I could run out to the mound and tell Dan McGinty, who was limping around out there in one work sock and one purple stocking and using a kid's glove. But I had the hanker.

"Hank's going," I told Hawg.

"Maybe yes and maybe no."

Perhaps he'll break too early, I was hoping, so that Dan could make the play at first. We'd all seen him do it, year after year, as if Dan McGinty's pitching would go on forever.

Sober stretched and threw. No steal, but the sinker was too deep in the dust for even Murph to label a strike. "Ball two!" he yelled, wringing a long moan from the Canby patrons. I felt it! Saw it before anyone else did. I saw Will Farnum's arm go back to lob the baseball to the mound as the disgruntled ball-two groan continued. And as Will threw the ball toward Sober, Hank Gitbo broke for second.

Delayed steal!

The moaners were still thinking about a two-and-oh count, something that didn't matter that much.

Then they saw Hank Gitbo's break from first. The groan turned too slowly to a yell of alarm. Sober caught the throwback and just stared at Murph who was spinning the wheel of his hand counter. Will Farnum, in a panic, waved toward second; but by the time Sober turned himself around by 180 degrees to look, Hank Gitbo coasted into second standing up.

Sober threw the ball into center field!

Gitbo took third and even allowed himself a healthy turn toward home before easing back to third base. Boo after boo was voiced by Canby citizens. No hit, and a man on third. Nobody out. So to make the situation worse, Sober walked Jerry Keen on two more pitches; a listless curve and a neck-high fastball that even I could have hit, had it been a foot lower.

As the hitter trotted toward first, Murph shrugged at Sober McGinty, as if to say: "It was darn close to through his dandruff. How can I call it a strike?"

"Ya still sleepin' it off, Sober?" yelled someone.

"Top of the first," snorted Hawg, "always been tough on Sober. Darn near every Sunday, and I known him twenty years. Closer to thirty."

"He'll settle down," I said.

"Sure," said Hawg. But there was little conviction in his voice, as though he doubted that McGinty could go the nine.

CHAPTER 6

"Here," said Hawg, clinking a pair of silver quarters into my hand. "Go fetch us each a hot dog and a bottle a' pop. Okay?"

"Sure," I said. "What flavor?"

"Grape for me if he's got it."

"What if he doesn't?"

"Then surprise me. Anything but cream soda."

Riley Shattuck, with the county's most unhygienic fingernails, handed me two hot dogs, two bottles of grape, and two nickels when he saw I waited for change. Walking real careful, I was trying not to drop or spill anything on the way back to the dugout, when I heard the crowd erupt into laughter. When I arrived to hand Hawg Hogarth his first dog and soda (which he would have every inning), I saw the source of the merriment. Out on the field, time had been called by Murph, in order to rid the diamond of a nineteenth participant, which happened to be Harv Winpenny's goat, Butler.

"Every doggone Sunday," sighed Hawg, his jowls already full and his hot dog half eaten in one bite.

"Butler's loose again?"

"Someday"—Hawg pointed at the brown and white goat with a half-empty bottle of Grape Crush —"I swear I'm gonna get me a shotgun and—" The teeth of his threat was lost in chewing.

Just beyond where Luke Fish (our shortstop) roamed, the grass seemed to be worth grazing, and Butler paused for refreshment. Luke threw his glove and Butler deftly ducked, pivoted, and strolled casually out in left field. In from his position came Harwood Mix, hoping that he could shoo Butler back toward Luke, or off to the sidelines. Several spectators crossed the foul line in a helpful effort to corner Butler, a goat who grazed often in Durkee's Lot and no doubt felt at home here.

"Go on! Git!"

"Beat it, Butler."

"Scram, ya cussed critter!"

"Hyah! Hyah!"

Butler moved, but in circles. Although he was a very large billy goat, he was amazingly agile, his tiny hoofs dancing in place just long enough to entice Harwood Mix (who was not agile) to make a lunge for him. Butler's first few steps during each of his rushes for freedom were masteries in artful dodging, nimble enough to elude any and all attempts at grabbing his beard, hind leg, or horns. Apparently he had, only moments earlier, heard the excitement in Durkee's Lot and meandered over to investigate, intending to enjoy liberty while he appreciated the national pastime.

Everybody looked around in order to place all of the blame on Harv Winpenny, yet Butler's owner seemed not to be in attendance.

"Go on, Butler!"

Milt Hewlitt (a rooter, not a player) threw a shoe, striking Butler on the flank. For a second or two, I thought for sure that Butler was going to charge Milt, horns first. But he didn't. Calmly, he lowered his head and plunged his nose into the shoe, and ate the tongue.

"Hey," shouted Milt, "he can't do that!"

"He's doing it," said Harwood.

The shoe tongue did not, it soon became obvious, quite agree with even Butler's determined digestive system or meet his relaxed dietary standards. This was unusual. Over the years in Canby, a variety of articles had sunk into that billy goat's stomach, never to rise again, passing into the lower regions and eventually dropping to lower altitudes, helping in altered form to green the grass of Durkee's Lot and to bloom its daisies. To my recollection, Butler had once eaten a helping of String Pendle's bicycle basket, several yards of Kirby Stinnet's garden hose (including the nozzle), most of the upholstery off the bench seat of Mahlon Bojanski's blue pickup truck, one of my

dolls, plus a loop of Gladice Appling's clothesline along with two clothespins and the black panties that she'd sent away for. All the way by mail order from Hollywood. Butler had ingested several sections of the Burlington *Free Press,* the Rutland *Herald,* and the Bennington *Banner* as well as the collar off Lick Donovan's watchdog, Pershing.

Lick always said that Persh wasn't afraid of man nor beast. Yet I figured Pershing met his match when he crossed paths with Butler Winpenny, a billy goat whose disposition was not as varied as his diet.

Butler's comprehensive menu was a common fact in Canby, I was thinking, as I saw the last of that shoe tongue disappear into Butler's mouth. Then, just as Milt Hewlitt (his other shoe still on his foot) ran forward, Butler quietly lowered his soft little nose into Milt's shoe . . . and threw up.

"Dang you, Butler!"

Apparently relieved, the goat trotted off, veering off toward center field, while Milt tried to decide on whether to reclaim his fouled footwear or leave it lie.

"Hey," yelled Murph the umpire, "that's your shoe, ain't it, Milt?"

"Nope," lied Milt, which was sort of silly, as there stood Milt Hewlitt wearing only half the pair.

"Hell it ain't! Get it off the field."

"Now?"

The shoe was a sorry sight, so bad that hardly a soul in town could have picked up that shoe without a long-handled shovel. As he limped (shoe, sock, shoe, sock) off the outfield grass, Milt Hewlitt held his shoe at an arm's length with one hand, holding his nose with the other.

"And it doesn't even have a tongue," he wailed, his voice almost in tears.

Hawg was chuckling.

So was I. To be truthful about it, I never did cotton to Milt Hewlitt a whole lot, seeing as he served as Canby's truant officer, which made what happened to his footwear even funnier. And now that Milt had reclaimed his shoe, I had to wonder (as I giggled) what his plans were for it. Now that he had recovered it, he didn't seem to know what to do with it; whether to just walk around carrying a shoe for the rest of Sunday, or to dig a hole and bury the pesky thing.

It was obvious that the fellows with whom Milt had been sitting did not want the shoe among them. "Get rid of it!" came a request that sounded more like a demand.

"Nobody's gonna catch that animal," sighed Hawg.

"Nope," I agreed, "not unless Butler wants catching."

"And he no-way don't."

Years back, when I had the chicken pox, I threw up twice, and I can't say I felt very good about the business either time. Yet upchucking seemed to put

Butler in a winsome mood, as he kicked up his heels, pausing to chew up a discarded matchbook cover along with a shiny object that I couldn't identify.

"What's he eating?"

"Bottle cap," said Hawg.

"Won't it make him sick?"

"Yup."

As we watched Butler alternately dispose of discarded litter and dodge away from those who were intent on ejecting him from the playing field, it apparently had its affect on Hawg's own hunger.

"Hey," he said flipping me another quarter, "ya wanna fetch me one more dog?"

"Okay."

"And hit me again on the grape. You want another? I'll spring."

"Naw. Thanks anyhow."

Hawg demolished his second intake of nourishment, punctuating its entrance into his system with an exit of gas.

"Lookit that dang goat," he said, as Butler gnawed at a paper napkin. "If it wasn't for him, we'd have junk all over this doggone place."

On third, Hank Gitbo waved his arms, shouting at Butler, while his running mate on first, Jerry Keen, did likewise. So did Vernal Klaus, our second sacker. In school, Karl Klaus sat right beside me, and also played short on our team. They owned goats, most of which I knew by name, so I figured Vernal would

have better luck. But not even he could convince
Butler to vacate. People were honking their horns in
the row of cars along the first-base line, and along
third.

Butler, and Hawg Hogarth, just ate.

A real manager, Hawg. Never got excited, whether
we lost or won. And if Sober arrived in sorry shape
for a Sunday game, as he always did and had for
many a season, Hawg accepted McGinty's hangover
as just one eccentricity of a pitcher's personality. I
doubt if Hawg would have hoisted himself up off the
bench even if he saw Butler Winpenny eat home
plate.

"Geez," he said, "it's three o'clock."

I figured I knew that Hawg was only counting the
minutes until his next Grape Crush and frankfurter.
Between the two of them, Hawg and Butler must
have chewed up half of Vermont.

"Why doesn't somebody do something?" yelled
Murph, his umpire's mask pushed up on top of his
head. Our catcher, Will Farnum, wore his mask the
same way.

Butler was grazing.

"Lookit him," hollered Murph. "Eating the
outfield clover like it was Monday."

Hawg turned to me. "You seen Pook?"

"He's usually here."

"Yeah, but you seen his car?"

"Not me."

"Heck."

Pook Rosetti was the town constable of Canby. Other than being half owner in the Army-Navy store, he shot a mean stick of pool (according to Sober McGinty), issued licenses to hunt and fish, and served as the local law. Town constable was an elected office and Pook not once in his long history on the force ever arrested anyone.

Law never had been any great concern in Canby. People usually did what they doggone pleased, and as long as it didn't wake up the neighbors, create too pungent an odor, disrupt the domestic tranquility, or ruin the horizon, Vermonters lived and let live.

"Hey, watch it!"

The center fielder for the Canby Catfish was our team speedster, Harry O'Toole, who was now approaching Butler slowly and stealthily from the rear.

"Watch it!"

Fans were yelling words of caution, making me wonder whether they were trying to warn Harry or Butler. The old billy goat's head was lowered as he contentedly filled his mouth with the timothy of Durkee's Lot. Closer and closer crept Harry O'Toole. All was silent.

"Get him," some nearby observer whispered.

That's when I spotted Florence Klaus, Vernal's wife, running out on the field, holding a short length of rope. On the lower end of the rope was Agnes, one of their nanny goats. About the time I saw

Florence, Butler spotted Agnes. I'd be hard put to describe Agnes as fetching or fragrant, but she was apparently pleasing to Butler's discerning eye, and nose. They all (Florence Klaus, Agnes, and Butler) trotted off the field in our direction.

"Thanks a lot, Flo," yelled Murph to Mrs. Klaus.

"Men!" I heard her snort in disgust.

CHAPTER 7

Jack Gitbo, center fielder for the Wiggin Warriors, hit third in their batting order. As he strutted to the plate, Canby booed him.

"S'funny," said Hawg.

"What's funny?" I asked him.

"Jack swings the biggest bat they got. Old Joe Gitbo used to bat him fourth, in cleanup, and today he's hittin' third spot. Ya know, I never noticed, and I been lookin' at their batting order for an hour."

"Dan told me about that," I said.

"You mean Sober? How'd *he* know?"

"Not about Jack. But last week or the week before, we were talking about long-ball hitters in the top of the order."

"So?" asked Hawg.

"Well, it made sense to Sober to have your best slugger hit third instead of fourth."

"Maybe he's right," shrugged Hawg.

"Maybe so."

"Who am I to question Injun Joe Gitbo or McGinty?"

Ball one, with runners on first and third, I figured Sober McGinty wasn't going to give Jack Gitbo a fat pitch. He'd just work the corners.

"That's it, Dan," I yelled out, hands cupping my mouth. "Serve him up his junk."

Hawg snorted. "That's okay. But three more hunks a junk and they got full bases and we got no outs."

Ball two. Sober's hook broke wide, and I thought for sure that Jerry Keen would break for second to draw a throw from Will Farnum. Jerry only bluffed a run, and Will faked a throw to second, trying to bait Hank Gitbo to cut loose from third and try home so they could trap him.

"No dice," said Hawg.

Ball three brought a moan from the crowd. Before Sober took his stretch for the fourth pitch, I saw Jack look over his shoulder at Old Joe in the dugout. What'll I do now, Pa? If the old manager flashed him a take sign, I never saw it.

Strike one, and the crowd hooted like it was a surprise.

"Big deal," said Hawg. "He'll be swinging away on the next one."

"For sure."

Our dugout was located along the start of the base line to first, and set back about thirty-five feet into foul territory. We looked across home plate at third

where Hank Gitbo took his lead in our direction. He looked fast, and was.

"You see what I see?" I asked Hawg.

"Whatcha got, Babe?"

"Hank Gitbo."

"Yeah?"

"See his feet. He's on the chalk line."

"Yeah!" Hawg pushed his purple cap forward over his eyes, as he scratched the thick gray hair on his neck. "I wonder how come Injun Joe don't move him outside the line."

"Maybe we'll be lucky," I said, "if Jack pulls. Does he?"

Hawg nodded. "He mostly hits to left."

We got a break. Manufacturing one heck of a big motion, like he was going to fast-ball the hitter, Dan McGinty threw his change-up and it took forever. Good pitch. Jack Gitbo swung his bat too early, getting way out in front of what would have been strike two.

Crack!

Hickory hit horsehide. And from his bold lead off third base, Hank Gitbo came down the line. A ground ball hit the chalk halfway toward third, took a mean hop, and bounced off Hank's leg. He was in fair territory, an automatic out, and as the spent ball dribbled toward the mound, Sober flipped it on a neat pivot to second and got the front runner, Jerry Keen, by three steps. There followed a dispute about a dead ball, but Murph ruled it as two away.

Two out, and even with Jack Gitbo safe on first, the Canby crowd came to life. Jack's hit might have been foul, and Hank died on third because he should have been off the bag but not on fair turf. I saw Hank limp into their crowded dugout and Old Joe scowl at him, just as Keen (out number two) joined them. The next hitter was Oscar Sanchez, a new player.

"Sanchez," said Hawg.

"Where'd they get *him?*"

"A ringer. Ain't nobody named Sanchez who lives in Wiggin that I know of."

"Do you know everybody there?"

"Not everybody. But my wife's old lady lives in Wiggin," said Hawg, "and *she* knows everything in town. Knows it and tells it. And I never heard her say Sanchez, but she sure mentioned everybody else."

Sanchez, whose history was yet a mystery to Hawg Hogarth's mother-in-law, popped up behind the plate. Will Farnum backpeddled, mitt on his left, mask in his right hand, as he became sure of where the ball would fall. Dropping his mask in the dust, Will made the catch, and Jack Gitbo died on first. In every car, Canby horns were happy.

"Holy Hannah," sighed Hawg, as the Catfish trotted our way, "I never thought Sober'd work out of that jam."

"I did."

I moved out of the dugout to make room for the players coming in from the field, and also to flash a relieved smile back at Aunt Hobart, who winked back as if to say we were lucky to be out of that inning. We sure were, I thought, watching a kid hang a goose egg on the scoreboard.

On the field of Durkee's Lot, the Warriors threw a few practice throws to first, while their pitcher, Sherman Gitbo, took his warm-up deliveries. Even though he had the shortest walk to our dugout (other than our catcher), Sober McGinty was last to reach the bench. He spat in my direction as if to say howdy.

"Good hurling, McGinty."

"Thanks, Babe."

"Dan, you had any breakfast or anything?"

"Nope. Can't pitch on a full stomach." He squatted down beside me, leaning his number seven against the edge of the dugout wall. I could see the sweat coming through the crown of his purple cap. His hands were still shaky.

"How'd my glove work out? Too small, huh?"

"Fine, Babe, just real fine. I sure do appreciate letting me borrow it."

"A real honor." I smiled at him.

"Brother! I sure do hope I don't have to hit this inning."

"You feeling poorly?"

"I ain't exactly prime."

"You'll come around, Dan."

"Always do. I can't let *you* down." As he gave one of my pigtails a yank, he made his train-whistle hoot.

"Never have yet." I hit his bent knee with my fist to tell him to hang in there.

"What we need on this here ball club," he said, "is a relief pitcher. I can pitch every Sunday, sure and all that, but we oughta have a backup. All we got is Jake. And he ain't even here yet."

Jake Broda was what Hawg referred to as a utility man. Infield or outfield, Jake was comfortably at home in as many corners of Durkee's Lot as Butler, the goat.

"Dan?"

"I hear ya."

"You think Jake Broda can pitch?"

"A little. He really ain't what you'd call a pitcher."

"What would you call him?" I asked Sober.

"A thrower."

"Has he got any stuff?"

"Yup, and it's all down the middle."

"Honest?"

"Oh, Jake can break a curve once a blue moon, if he's pitching for batting practice."

"How about today?"

"No way, Babe. If you put Jake on a Sunday mound and he hears all of Canby yelling his name and he looks at the plate and sees some young bronk like Jack Gitbo who can knock the hide off the string, he gets choked."

"How come?"

"Just does. He tensions up. And it don't got to be a slugger like Big Jack. Even ya put a no-hit guy up at the plate, some gink who couldn't whack an elephant's ass with a snow shovel, Jake Broda would see this here joker as Ty Cobb."

"No kidding?"

"Yup."

"Guess we're stuck with you, McGinty."

"Reckon we are."

Gil Haskin led off. Sherman Gitbo threw him a ball and from the roar of the Canby reaction, you'd a' thought we won the World Series.

"Make 'em be in there, Gil," mumbled Hawg.

Sherman Gitbo's second pitch was a high hummer, and Gil's swing undercut it by nearly a foot.

"See that, Babe?" said Sober.

"He missed it."

"Yeah, but when you're at the plate as a hitter, remember this, Babe. Wait for your pitch and then take your cut at the *top* half of the ball."

"Why?"

"Most hitters swing low."

"How come they do?"

"Gravity. The heft of the bat pulls their swing down, on account of they oughta get the bat back with the right elbow held up high. Force it up."

"What'll that do?"

Sober spat. "Well, for one thing, it'll level out your swing so's your cut don't just take a Baltimore chop at the ball as if you wanta drive it into home plate instead out at center."

"Is that all?"

"A level swing moves your bat *through* the ball instead of at it, and ups your chances to connect."

"I'll remember, Dan."

Strike two.

"He swings too hard," said Sober. "Don't ever try to kill it, Babe. Just meet it, and let the speed of the pitch do the rest. The important thing is not to hit or walk, but to *get* on base. When kids play baseball, I tell ya what wins games, Babe, and it don't have a thing to do with a ball or a bat or a glove. What wins is heads-up base running."

Gil Haskin looked at a third strike, then he looked at Murph who shrugged an apology as if to remind Gil that Sherm Gitbo had grooved a pitch and nobody had the brains to put wood on a perfect strike.

On the first pitch, Luke Fish bounced out to short, and we watched Jerry Keen make the play by going to his right. From deep in the hole, he backhanded the grounder and made the long throw to Oscar Sanchez who made the long stretch, and Luke was out by a step. Against his will, Murph, who had trotted down the first-base line to call the play, threw his right arm in the air. Any closer and we all knew Murph's call would have come not from his eyesight but from his heart.

Or his wallet.

Harwood Mix really tagged one, but it was high and the breeze carried the ball in from the center-field fence where Jack Gitbo, ankle-deep in poison ivy, made an easy catch.

Sober limped out into the heat.

CHAPTER 8

"Pinch me," said Hawg, "on account of I don't really believe it."

"Believe what?" I asked.

"What I think I just heard."

Before I could ask him what he was hearing, I heard it, too. Every ear in Durkee's Lot heard it, as well as everyone in the county and half of Vermont. Coming our way, a low scream building up to a medium scream and ending with a wail that was pitched higher than Heaven. Hawg and I both came out of our empty dugout to check it out. I couldn't see a thing except all the action on the field had been suspended.

"Doggone them guys," said Hawg with a deep sigh.

"What guys?"

"Ya know," he shook his head, "they told me they'd tool that dang-fool contraption over this afternoon and show it off."

"Who are they?"

"The Hoover guys and their new engine."

Hoover was the closest town to Canby going south. Standing next to Hawg Hogarth, I was wondering what the scream was until I saw the big red monster pull into Durkee's Lot. Biggest hook-and-ladder machine I ever saw, and the longest, and redder than Satan's blush.

"Damn them guys," said Hawg.

Aboard their shiny new fire truck rode about a dozen fellows, all in their navy-blue uniforms, and I figured it had to be the Hoover Volunteer Fire Company out in full dress. Some of them wore their red fire helmets on backward, or sideways, making it rather obvious that the membership had celebrated the Four of July on beverages with more personality than Grape Crush.

Coming through the gate, the big engine never stopped. With a driver in front and a second driver in the rear, the Hoover Hook-and-Ladder Number Two (with gold lettering) roared out onto the diamond and raced around, kicking up small twisters of tan infield dust, all claxon horns blowing. Sure was deafening. Finally, when a Hoover volunteer fell off as the long red engine rounded third base, they brought the thing to a wheezing halt, smothering home plate.

"Their new toy." Hawg shook his head.

"Sure is big," I said.

"Lord pity Hoover if they ever have a fire."

Fans swarmed out to see the new engine, while lit-

tle old Murph just stood, fists on the hips of his black suit, as if he wondered how he'd ever get the Hoover fellows to shift their hooting assembly into less conspicuous quarters. Several of the flame-eaters from Hoover refreshed themselves from bottles inside brown paper bags. Others had brown and green bottles of beer and ale.

Out on the mound, Sober McGinty licked his dry lips.

"I don't believe it," said Hawg. He turned to me with another silver quarter.

"Another dog and a grape?"

"If ya don't mind, Babe."

"I don't mind."

Over a score of other baseball faithfuls had the same idea, and Riley Shattuck's raw hot dogs and warm soda were never more in demand. People pushed in front of me and, after I made Hawg's purchase, jostled me before I could execute a clean getaway from the pop-sticky and mustard-smeared counter. As I was jostled, a spurt of Grape Crush stained the front of my uniform, near the B of CANBY, but I didn't pay such a minor mishap too much attention, since the spreading purple puddle on my shirt sort of matched my purple cap and socks.

As I handed Hawg his third snack, the corner of my eye picked out Sober among the flock of admirers surrounding Hoover's red fire engine. I saw him handing a brown paper bag back to one of the Hoover firemen. Then he wiped his mouth with the back of his hand. I wanted to run out and tell off Dan McGinty and say it loud and proper, but instead I figured best I tend to my own business. So I just knelt down to straighten up our fan of bats as though I didn't care how my friend McGinty pickled his stomach. I just pounded the dirt with my fist.

"Geez," said Murph, "fun's fun and all that, but would you guys move this blessed rattletrap so we can play a little baseball?"

With some cranking, some words that my father said sometimes when he was under the Hudson, and no small measure of fanfare, Hoover Hook-and-Ladder Number Two managed to cough up a start and wheeze off the field.

"I still don't believe it," said Hawg, his mouth fully occupied with the last of his Riley Shattuck delicacy which he sent plummeting into his iron-clad digestive system with a pronounced gulp. Hawg's belch sounded like a suddenly unclogged sink.

"Believe it," I said.

"I told them guys," said Hawg, "if they brought that darn thing in here, they'd be the guests of the Canby Jail."

"Play ball," said Murph.

Play resumed and we saw Dan McGinty face Howard Gitbo, Bert Dilworth, and Andy Salvatore.

One, two, three, and McGinty struck out the side. His hook was working and his fast ball looked like a hummer.

When the Catfish came into the dugout, Will Farnum slipped the sponge into his mitt.

"How's his stuff, Will?" I asked our catcher, while Dan helped himself to a dipper of water from the bucket.

"Growing."

"Honest?"

"His last fast ball near to busted my hand."

Harry O'Toole took the first pitch, a ball, and singled the next up the middle, through the box and over the bag. Jack Gitbo came up with it and threw easily to second when he saw Harry take his turn at first.

"Lay one down," Hawg told Vernal Klaus.

But the first pitch to Vernal from Sherm Gitbo was high, and he saw Vern facing around as if to bunt. At third, his glove ready, Hank Gitbo crept in; itching to throw out the possible force at second and get the front runner, as Sober had done in the first inning.

Vernal bunted, fouling the ball off his foot, so that time had to be called by Murph while Vern danced around, telling everybody about what we saw, except him. Out on the mound, Sherman Gitbo checked first and then delivered.

Pitchout!

There was no way that Vernal could have put wood to it, and the wide pitch thudded into Gus Gitbo's mitt, catching a surprised Harry O'Toole halfway between first and second.

Hawg said a dirty word.

Harry tried to scamper back to first on the rundown, but the throw from Howard Gitbo to Oscar Sanchez nailed him. He was tagged. Harry came back to the dugout, sweating, and took his place in the shade.

"Ain't yer fault," Sober told him.

Old Joe Gitbo, I decided, had just outsmarted us and gambled on the pitchout. Gambled and won. We lost.

Vernal popped up.

Norm Goodnew, our right fielder, foul-tipped a third strike which Gus Gitbo's mitt hung onto, and our side was retired. One hit, but no runs. Across the plate, on the other side, I saw Gus Gitbo unclip his red shinguards and then swing three bats in order to loosen up as the next hitter.

Ball one.

I saw Sober throw his sinker, and it wasn't much of a pitch. Will Farnum had to dig for it, and it got away from him. Lucky for us, Wiggin had no base runners, or the advance would have been a piece of cake.

Ball two. Dan went to his knuckler which weaved worse than his walk out to the mound. Ball three.

"Get it over," I heard Hawg say. "Please."

Strike one, and Gus was taking all the way. But then Dan added a little on his fast ball and Gus couldn't get around on it. On the full-counter, Gus slapped it to right for a clean single. Up came the pitcher, Sherman Gitbo.

Ball one.

"See them two?" said Hawg to me.

"Which ones?"

"Sherm and Gus."

"What about 'em?"

"Brothers. Years back, I was up in Wiggin, coon-doggin' after their sister, Dolores, and them two guys beat the by-George out of me."

"They shouldn't of done that," I said.

"Yeah," said Hawg, "they shoulda."

Ball two. The crowd was uneasy on the planks of their benches, and when Murph indicated by no more than a shrug that Dan's slider missed for ball three, the mumble of sour talk began to build. Somebody smashed a bottle.

Ball four.

"Crap!" said Hawg. "He walks their doggone pitcher."

Across the way, in the Warrior dugout I saw old Joe Gitbo rub his hands, delighted with current events. The Warriors on first and second broke on Dan's first pitch, and Hank Gitbo swung late, to hit behind the runner from first. As our second sacker, Vernal, scooted to his right to cover the bag, what should have been "a routine ground ball," as Sober often called it, bounced happily out into right.

Gus Gitbo scored.

Not because of his burning speed from second, but on account of he had such a jump on the ball when Hank hit safely through the hole on the hit and run. Sherman Gitbo, wearing his jacket to keep his pitching arm hot, took third on Norm Goodnew's late throw home.

"One to nothin'," said Hawg.

Jerry Keen waited, and Hank Gitbo stole second. Will Farnum did not throw. If he had, Sherman Gitbo would have cut loose from third. From the anxious look on his face, he was smelling home plate.

"S'okay, Dan," I yelled to the mound.

"Get the hitter," said Hawg.

"First is open," I said.

"So what do you want me to do?" said Hawg. "Rent it out like a room? Keen's no hitter, and maybe McGinty can lean on him some. Okay with you?"

"Sure," I said.

Jerry Keen popped up in foul ground just outside first base, an easy out for Gil Haskin.

"One away," I said.

As Jack Gitbo, their best long-ball hitter came to the plate, Hawg looked at me. "First is still open."

"Yup," I said, "wide open."

"Well, ya think I oughta put him on?"

"I would."

"Babe, we're a run behind. To tell ya the truth, if it was up to me, I wouldn't give an intentional walk to my own mother."

"Is big Jack Gitbo your mother?"

"No," said Hawg, "he sure ain't."

"I'd put him on and pitch to Sanchez."

"You win. But I don't like it, on account that Dan's control is hot and cold. I don't like it, Babe, but I'll put Jack Gitbo on."

Sober McGinty shrugged his shoulders as Hawg Hogarth pointed toward first. Four intentional balls later and Jack Gitbo trotted down the base line, amid boos from Wiggin rooters who wanted big Jack to swing away with two on.

With the ball in the glove (my glove) and his purple cap in his right hand, Dan McGinty wiped the July sweat off his brow with the right sleeve of his uniform. A tug of his cap and he was ready to face Oscar Sanchez. He threw Oscar a strike, and then walked him on four straight, forcing in a run.

Into home came Sherman Gitbo, walking, stamping the white plate with his cleats.

"Two runs in," said Hawg.

CHAPTER 9

"Ya see?" Hawg turned to me.

"I see."

"It don't pay to walk a man and load up the bases. I know, I know . . . with one out, if he hits into a double play we can retire the side, unless first base is open."

"Sometimes," I said.

"So we load 'em up and Sober walks in a run. We was between the rock and the hard place."

Howard Gitbo popped high to deep short, an effortless play for Luke Fish. "Two away, gang," Luke yelled to the infield, meaning no play at the plate. On a ground ball, the Catfish could take the easy play and throw out the hitter at first.

As he faced Bert Dilworth, Sober threw a strike and then another. Getting that far ahead of the hitter, with the bases loaded, pleased the Canby crowd. They hooted and hollered their encouraging support out to our pitcher.

"Now work him," said Hawg.

"That's what I'd do," I said. "Waste one. Throw a piece of junk at him and see if he bites."

"Yeah," said Hawg.

Sober wasted one. His sinker sunk. As the ball dug into the dirt ahead of the plate, I saw Will Farnum try to quick-hop it; but it bounced by, rolling all the way (thirty feet) to the backstop. All three runners advanced and Hank Gitbo trotted in from third.

"Three to zip," moaned Hawg.

"It's okay, Dan," I yelled. But he probably didn't hear my holler as the Canby people were groaning, and the Wiggin folks were honking their horns.

"Bear down out there, Sober," yelled Hawg, "and put some juice on that apple."

Sober bore down, striking out Bert Dilworth, allowing the Canby Catfish to return to a shady seat in the dugout. Sober McGinty's face was wet and dripping. The old number seven on the back of his shirt was a purple island in a sopping sea of sweat. He sat down beside me, his mouth open, and I just said nothing as I listened to his breathing. Getting up, I found his jacket to drape around his shoulders.

"Everybody hits," said Hawg Hogarth. "Whaddya say we bat around?"

Unlikely, I was thinking.

"Babe," said Hawg, "go tell Harley we need some music. That's what the goshdang band is for, to fire us guys up. Okay?"

"Okay," I said.

Harley Romano directed the Canby Silver-Cornet Band, and also played the melody on his silver cornet for almost every number. When I got to the bandstand, Harley looked warmer and wetter than any of the athletes. Harley was short and plump with a face as purple as a plum, especially after a cornet solo. He smiled his purple smile at me.

"Hi there, Babe."

"Howdy, Mr. Romano." I never called him Harley as he was also the music teacher at Canby Central School.

"Hot enough for ya?" he asked.

"Sure is. Hawg wants the band to play some more."

"We already played every piece we know three times. That's fifteen numbers."

"All I know is, Hawg asked me to ask the band to play. As a favor."

Harley wiped his purple face with a white hanky. "Well, you can go tell Hawg Hogarth that if he wants music, best he climb up on this rickety bandstand, sit in the hot sun, and play this darn cornet for a couple of hours and see how *he* likes it. I'm not getting paid for this, you know."

"I know. Neither am I."

"Murph gets a dollar."

"Yes, I guess so."

"I s'pose," said Harley Romano, his chubby fingers pumping the three little valves on his silver horn,

"that folks in Canby think that it takes more training to umpire a baseball game than it does to master a musical instrument."

"Well, I guess we all like your music, Mr. Romano. I sure do."

"Do you think we get free hot dogs? Like heck."

"If it was up to me," I said, "everybody who plays in the Silver-Cornet Band would get free dogs and free pop."

"You're a nice little girl, Babe."

"Thank you, sir."

"Doesn't your pa play a horn?"

"Years back, he used to play the tuba."

As I said it, Olly Finch, who held a large and imposing silver tuba in his lap, glared at me as though it was my plan to redo the one-man tuba section, installing Alf Babson in Olly's chair. His mouth tightened, which created a dent in his cheek, and it sort of matched the dent inside the big golden bell of his tuba.

"Huh!" snorted Olly.

"Hey now, Olly," said Harley, "nobody said your hornblowing wasn't up to snuff. I was just asking Babe here about her father's hobbies." He turned back to me. "Does he play anything else?"

"Mostly he tinkers on his Hudson." I should have said *under* it.

"Oh, a mechanic?"

"No," I said, "but we wish he was."

The band all laughed, except Olly who seemed to hug his tuba a bit closer to his heart.

"Well," said Harley, "you can tell Hawg Hogarth that we'll do one more number, and then we have to pack up. After all, some of us have to play at the Revival tonight."

"I forgot," I said. "What are you going to play?"

"Tonight?"

"Yes," I nodded.

"Tonight we play *hymns*. We'd play some now, but it wouldn't be too proper for a ball game, eh?"

"No, I don't guess it would."

As the Canby Silver-Cornet Band thrashed its way through "Our Director" for the fourth time, I hurried back to the dugout and hunkered down in the dirt in front of Sober McGinty. Lead-off hitter for the inning was our third sacker, Cecil Snow.

Strike one.

"Sherm looks good," said Sober. "Best I seen him work. Strong and steady."

Strike two.

"Don't let him kid you, Dan. His mound's as hot as yours."

"Sure is a scorcher," said McGinty, his teeth tearing off a healthy chaw of Mail Pouch.

My nose caught one whiff of his breath, and it sure wasn't Grape Crush. I wondered if Dan had put as much as a hot dog in his stomach since last night. Like he knew what I was thinking, he put his big old hands on my shoulders and rubbed my neck with his thumbs. "Stay loose, Babe."

"Me, I'm always loose."

But I could still smell the Saturday on his breath, so sour that I wanted to turn around and cuff some sense into him, sort of beat up on him (real easy) until he took the pledge to quit drinking. Booze and baseball, he had once confessed to me, don't mix. "In fact, whiskey don't mix with money or marriage or one doggone thing in a man's life," he had said.

As I was thinking about Dan McGinty's problem, I wasn't really in tune to what was happening in front of my eyes, out on the sun-bleached diamond of Durkee's Lot.

Crack!

The bat meeting the ball sort of woke me up as the roar of the hometown rooters welcomed the clean single that Cecil Snow had knocked over third. In left, Bert Dilworth's peg to second held up Cecil at first.

"Bunt." I heard Hawg's whisper to Will Farnum, who had kicked off his purple shinguards, knowing it was his inning to bat.

"You bet," answered Will Farnum.

"We gotta push in a score," said Sober.

"We sure do," I said.

"Three runs down." Sober grunted up off the bench and swung a pair of Louisville Slugger bats.

Ball one.

At first base, Oscar Sanchez was flapping his glove at Sherm Gitbo, as if he expected a move on Cecil who was hugging the bag. His lead was far from daring, no more than three steps, as Cecil was no speed merchant.

Ball two, a pitchout, but Cecil wasn't going. This made me figure that Injun Joe Gitbo had by this time instructed his pitcher to work on Will Farnum's bat.

Strike one.

"Geez," said Hawg, "he shoulda went for it."

Hank Gitbo, expecting the bunt, was creeping in close from third, his glove ready. And then Will Farnum laid one down, a perfect bunt that danced along the uneven chalk line toward first but stayed fair. Sherman Gitbo's only play was to first. Even though Will was out by the length of a Greyhound bus, the sacrifice worked. Safe on second, and snugly in scoring position on a single, was Cecil Snow.

With his crooked old gait, Dan McGinty walked slowly to the plate; taking his time so that Cecil Snow on second would get a few moments more of breather. Sober knew all the tricks, every one. As he left the dugout, the Canby crowd as well as the Wiggin crowd reacted with mixed appreciation. The Catfish were trailing by three runs and plenty of that was Sober's doing.

"Get a hit!" someone yelled.

"Yeah, surprise me, McGinty."

"Open yer eyes, if you can stand the pain."

Sunday in Durkee's Lot always attracted the local wits of Canby. It was part of the game, and Dan McGinty had heard all the wisecracks and had been the target of many a poke. Both kinds, the cruel and the comical. It would take more than the loudmouths on any bench to rattle old Sober. Before stepping into the batter's box, McGinty looked at Sherman Gitbo out on the mound, then Sober let a brown stream of tobacco juice fly in Sherman's direction. As if to tell the Warrior hurler to throw his best stuff.

The fans loved it.

Sherman Gitbo didn't. Ball one, high and inside, the kind that a pitcher calls a brush-back and a hitter calls (more accurately) a beanball. I was praying Dan would duck in time, figuring Sherman Gitbo just might waste one inside to make Sober dance. Ball two, as Sherm's curve missed. Strike one, with Sober taking all the way. He wanted to run up the count chewing Mail Pouch while Sherman Gitbo worked in the heat.

"Sherm's no spring chicken," said Hawg.

"How old is he?"

"Well, he ain't as old as McGinty, but he must be pushing forty."

Strike two.

"He's *gotta* swing away," said Hawg. "With first

base open, no grounder is gonna double us up. But he's gotta swing the timber."

Ball three. A full count on Sober. Just what he wanted to do, I guessed, make Gitbo work and throw in the heat. Sherm delivered, and it was a good pitch, but Sober fouled it back.

CHAPTER 10

"Sober's still alive," said Hawg.

In the heat of the mound, Sherman Gitbo wiped his wet face with the red sleeve of his underjersey, looking over at the dugout as if to ask Old Joe what to throw next. Sherman's questioning look did not escape at least one Canby fan:

"What'll I do now, Pa?" echoed over Durkee's Lot.

In response to the local wit, the other Canby fans took up the cry, and the tension of a three-two count with a runner on second was eased by fun-loving ridicule. This is part of baseball, I smiled to myself, and that's why this game is so doggone much a part of Babe Babson and living in Canby. It sure was great to be a bat girl for a nifty bunch of guys like the Catfish.

"Full count," Hawg reminded Sober.

Please, I was saying to Heaven, don't let Dan just stand there and look at a third strike. Even though

Murph couldn't call an honest hog, go for it if it's in there, Dan.

It was in.

McGinty stepped into the curve ball and placed one between first and second, a neat and clean single. As Cecil Snow's lead from second was long (seeing Sherm was a right-hander) his jump on the three-two pitch was a bit risky. Out in right, Andy Salvatore was in (as an opposite fielder ought to be) and came up with the ball faster than Rolly Jacob's terrier, just as Cecil turned third and saw Hawg waving him in. Cecil and the ball reached the plate at more or less the same time. He could have been safe, or out, but there was little doubt in Murph's biased, yet decisive, mind.

"Safe!"

Arms extended, Murphy indicated that the run scored, making it a three-one ball game. In a fury, Gus Gitbo, the Warrior receiver who had tagged Cecil possibly in time, ripped off his mask to bark at Murph. Dancing in the air in absolute joy, Cecil scampered toward our dugout. And one more thing occurred:

McGinty stole second.

"Lookit that old war horse," chuckled Hawg. "Runs like a pregnant buffalo, and he cops an extra base. That's what makes Sober McGinty such a heads-up ballplayer."

Out of the dugout came the red-and-black checkerboard shirt, deerskin pants, mocs, and crimson baseball cap of Injun Joe Gitbo. Never did he leave the visitor's dugout unless his Warriors were in a jam, or he didn't approve of one of Murphy's dubious decisions. One of which was the recent play at the plate. And as the Wiggin catcher turned to the old manager, up into the July afternoon, the cry arose once more:

"What'll I do now, Pa?"

Time was called. There was a long and verbal rhubarb at home plate, so out to second I trotted, carrying Sober's jacket. There was a slight breeze, and I sure didn't want what was left of Dan's arm to cool off, or cramp up.

"I don't need it, Babe."

"Yes, ya do."

"Okay," he stabbed his fist into the purple sleeve, "if it'll make ya feel any better. Nag, nag, nag."

"It'll make *you* feel better."

"I gotta feel better, Babe, on account there's no way I could feel any worse."

"Are you sick?"

"Just old."

"Go on! You're not old, McGinty."

"I ain't, huh?"

"Nah. Not you. Nobody's over the hill who can swipe second the way you did. You really can stretch a single."

"Like I tell ya, Babe. Them Wiggin goofs'll beat us

on the base lines unless we give 'em a bit of their own
what-for."

"Dan?"

"Yeah."

"You see the play at home?"

"I saw it."

"Did he make the tag on Cecil?"

"Appeared to me he did."

"Honest?"

"By a good half step. Murph's closer than I was,
so maybe he saw it different."

"I bet."

"Good old Murph," said Dan. "He's like a tenth
player. Instead of black, Murph oughta be in purple."

"Dan, are ya going to steal third?"

"You crazy?" He was still puffing from his scoot
from home to second. "I wouldn't make third by
Monday noon."

"Are you working tomorrow?"

"If I got the strength to punch in."

"What shift?" I started back toward the dugout.

"Three to eleven."

Almost every able-bodied male in town who wasn't
a farmer or a merchant was employed by the local
mill, the Canby Pulp Works. We didn't make paper
in town, just pulp, in flat gray sheets that were
shipped to finishing mills and thrown into what
Sober told me was called a beater. When I asked

him if it was something like Mama's egg beater, Dan said that beaters in a paper mill were a bit bigger, but the principle was the same. The beater looked more like the wheel on a steamboat, he said.

Dan McGinty's job at the Canby Pulp Works was in the chipper room, where he hooked cordwood into a chute and big blades chopped the logs to poker chips in only a second or two. I saw him work his job the day that our teacher, Miss Logan, took us on a tour through the Pulp Works.

I saw his lips that day say "Hi ya, Babe." But seeing as a chipper room is about the noisiest spot in the whole world, I couldn't hear a thing. With my hands over my ears, I just ran out of there.

"Play ball," we heard Murph command, as he decided to turn his back to the protesting from Gus and Injun Joe. The old man loped back into the Warrior dugout and Gus Gitbo dropped his mask over his face. I crouched just outside the Catfish dugout after I retrieved the bat that Sober had singled with, restoring it to its rightful rank in our fan of weaponry. I smiled back at Aunt Hobart who was eating a hot dog and motioned to ask if I wanted one. No thanks, I told her. Now that Sober was on second, I sure wasn't going to eat.

Gil Haskin was our next hitter.

But as he walked up to the plate, no one seemed to care whether or not Gil or Mel Ott was at bat for Canby. Right then, Durkee's Lot was invaded by a disorderly but joyful group of men in black trousers, white shirts, black hats, and draped in bunting of red and green. Several were armed with brass horns and drums, plus a giant flag also of three wide stripes . . . red, white, and green. Others carried what appeared to be baskets of straw from which a man suddenly drank deeply. Their large leader, a friendly fellow who seemed to be wearing several medals on his shirt, commanded that they play and sing along with their impressive entrance. The music was sour and off key, so bad that they made our Silver Cornets sound like the United States Marine Band. Their tune was nothing I had ever heard before, and surely not "Our Director."

"I'll be dipped," sighed Hawg.

"Who *are* those people?" Aunt Hobart yelled to me over the earsplitting din.

"I'll find out."

Hawg groaned, "Sons of Italy."

"The Sons of Italy," I yelled back at Aunt Hobart.

I'd forgotten about yesterday. Next to me in school sat one of my best friends, a kid named Angelo Morelli who had informed me (during practice this past week) that this coming Saturday, July third, had been named Italian-American Day.

"If yesterday was Italian-American Day," I asked Hawg, "how come they're parading again today?"

"It ain't again," said Hawg. "It's the same parade. Them guys ain't even been to bed yet."

As we talked, the crowd laughed and the Sons of Italy marched (out of step) around the bases, blowing their brasses and beating their drums (one bass and three snares), waving their banners and singing some sort of an anthem. One man marched close to our dugout and waved to Lick Donovan, shouting a happy greeting to him in a long Italiano sentence of which I understood not one word.

Lick just blinked. "Them guys is from out a' town," he observed.

But, as often was the case, Lick was mistaken.

A good quarter of Canby's citizens, or their parents, were born in Italy. (As Hawg phrased it, "of Eye-Talian persuasion.") At least once a winter I was invited to eat at Angelo's, where Mama Morelli served up platters of pasta the size of a manhole cover. Each bite was laced with garlic, bloodied with tomato sauce, and poxed with peppers, mushrooms, and goat cheese. Taking a bite of one of Papa Morelli's hot pepperonis was worse than having your throat cut.

It was then that I suddenly recognized the corpulent chap who now asked the Sons of Italy to execute what only vaguely resembled a column left as they marched from third to home plate, black shoes covered with dust, even though black trousers were several inches too long on almost every leg. He saluted and I remembered where he and I had met, and ate.

The big Italian-American was Angelo's very own
Uncle Albert.

I liked Uncle Albert. Even though he always
looked as though his trousers were about to drop.
They never did. He just wore his pants at half-mast.

"I'll be a son of . . ." Hawg paused.

"Italy?" I asked.

Shrugging, he shuffled toward the hot-dog establishment, prepared to partake further of those irre-
sistible morsels so meticulously prepared by the culi-
nary genius of Riley Shattuck.

Everyone in Durkee's Lot was waving to Uncle Albert and he waved back, smiling a wide white smile.
Lifting high the baggy pantlegs of his black trousers,
Uncle Albert pranced toward home plate, his arms
waving more or less in time with music that came
from an ensemble that could only have rehearsed in
the Canby Pulp Works chipper room.

"Ain't it awful," said somebody.

"Yeah," said his friend, "but great. At least it ain't
'Our Director.'"

Out of step to a man, on and on, around and
around Durkee's Lot marched the Sons of Italy,
banners flying and band playing as if each instru-
mentalist had a different tune in mind. Their music
had no beginning, no end, neither melody nor har-
mony. Only a dreadful yet delightful din. Every
member of the Sons of Italy seemed to be hideously

happy; no one, however, approaching the level of giggling glee equal to enormous Uncle Albert's.

As he went by, I could see his medals bounce, one of them covering what appeared to be a generous tomato stain on the front of his white shirt. I wanted to run out on the diamond to ask Uncle Albert what the medals were for, certainly not for either music or choreography. Possibly for enthusiasm.

Directly in the path of the Sons of Italy stood little Murph, legs planted wide, an umpire who looked suddenly determined, as though he fully intended to announce to the parading Italian-Americans that enough was enough, that yesterday was *their* day, and "Play ball!"

Murph was not a big man, but unfortunately Uncle Albert was. With an arc of his convivial arm and with a clatter of medals (one of which strangely resembled my Dick Tracy decoder), Albert Morelli swept Murph up as a madonna would lovingly hold a child and continued his parading without missing any more of the beat than had already been unanimously missed.

Fans were hysterically laughing, especially the players and the folks from Wiggin, as they saw Murph's face redden darker and darker as he was toted toward the pitcher's mound by Uncle Albert and the Sons of Italy.

The band played on, festooning the Four of July

atmosphere with flats and flags of red, white, and green. But upon reaching the mound, tragedy halted the parade, as Uncle Albert's dusty toe stubbed the white rubber. He pitched forward, dropping Murph and then (to worsen the indignity) fell on him. Murph screamed, Uncle Albert screamed, and all of Durkee's Lot screamed in hilarity. Tears ran down my cheeks I was laughing so hard, and I saw Aunt Hobart unpin her large hanky to wipe her eyes.

Hawg checked his pocket watch, then he turned to me and said, "This here Durkee's Lot ain't a ball field. You wanna know what this here place is, Babe?"

"What is it?" I asked him.

"It's Vermont's biggest open-air insane asylum."

CHAPTER 11

I couldn't quit laughing.

The madder Murph became and the redder his face grew, the funnier the whole day seemed to be, although I don't guess it's very much fun to have Uncle Albert drop you, then trip, and land on top of you . . . all at once. My sides hurt worse than a circus, and all of Hawg was laughing. Every pound. This was a bit unusual, as Hawg Hogarth seemed originally to be opposed to the Sons of Italy; at least he wasn't overjoyed at their arrival. So Hawg was chuckling, too, as folks like Uncle Albert are hard to hate.

"Know what, Babe?" said Hawg.

"No, what?"

"I think I'll walk over and ask Injun Joe Gitbo if I can spring for a couple a' grapes. You want one?"

"No thanks."

"And then, I best go see what ails Murph. I can't let anything happen to an umpire like him," said Hawg, "or we'll *never* beat them Wiggin guys."

In less than a minute, Hawg's mighty arm was around the shoulder of Joe Gitbo, and the two of them seemed to be enjoying the afternoon. People were all over the field, and the Sons of Italy seemed permanently encamped at the pitcher's mound, having rushed to the side of Uncle Albert, their fallen drum major; and to our flattened official, Murph.

"Hey!" I heard a lady say, "would ya take a gander at what just come through the gate."

We all looked.

I saw black horses pulling black wagons. One after another, into Durkee's Lot they came as though the place was theirs. Six wagons in all, each one black, and pulled by horses as black as sin on a Sabbath.

Turning quickly, I saw Aunt Hobart walking in my direction, so I trotted back to meet her. Side by side, Aunt Hobart and I stood on the grass between first-base line and the Catfish dugout, watching all those black wagons arrive. I sort of had me a hunch as to what it was and who they were, but I asked anyhow:

"Is—is that—?"

"Sure is," said Aunt Hobart. "It's the Revival."

As the the first driver, who was also dressed in black with a black stovepipe hat, pulled in his team of black horses, the wagon swung to one side and allowed me to read aloud the letters on the wagon, which said:

> JEHOVAH BIBLE & REVIVAL TENT
> & ORGAN SHOW.

"My stars, but you surely can read, Babe," said Aunt Hobart.

"That's because I'm a hard tryer."

"Who said so?"

"Miss Logan."

"Well," said Aunt Hobart, "seems to me Miss Logan knows her onions. Do you like your teacher?"

"Yeah," I said. "Miss Logan is real regular."

As we moved closer, Aunt Hobart and I, to get ourselves a cozier look, I could see that the same lettering was on both sides of all six wagons. The last three wagons turned a bit wide and didn't whoa until they pulled up away over the right-field foul line.

"I smell it," said Aunt Hobart.

"Smell what?"

"Trouble."

"What kind?"

"Territorial," said Aunt Hobart. "And it's the most natural instinct in man or beast."

"I don't quite understand," I told her.

"Babe," she said, "have you ever attempted to pour two gallons of cider into a one-gallon jug?"

Right then I knew what Aunt Hobart meant. "You figure that Durkee's Lot just might not be big enough for a baseball game and a Revival at the same time?"

"You got it." Aunt Hobart punched me. Not hard.

Looking over my shoulder, I saw a crowd of players and people at the mound, but could no longer see either Murph or Uncle Albert. But there wasn't a fight or anything. If there had been, I don't guess I'd want to miss it. Except not between Hawg and Uncle Albert. No chance of that. Hawg never lost his temper. He said he was just plain too big an ox to do dumb things.

One of the black wagons opened up like it was sort of a stage, with an organ and a pulpit, and some round silver dishes that probably took up collection.

"Do they take your offering at Revival, just like in church?" I asked Aunt Hobart.

"Count on it. Babe, there are three things in this world of ours that never can seem to run without money."

"What three things?"

"Politics, poker, and a prayer meeting."

As she said it, I sort of held my breath, as though I'd heard something blasphemous. I guess she noticed my mouth fall open.

"Did I shock you, Babe?"

"Sort of."

"I keep forgetting that you're only twelve. Yes, there's a lot about religion that I don't especially cotton to. But then again, a good Saving makes it all worthwhile."

As we all crowded around the wagon that had suddenly become a kind of a play-acting stage, we saw a lady in black and gray sit down at the organ, and in less than a breath, one of my favorite hymns

came swelling out of the box. We all started to sing "There's a Golden Garden in the Bye and Bye." Some folks who couldn't sing clapped their hands in time to the music.

"She sure can play," I said. "Who is she?"

"That lady," said Aunt Hobart, "is Sister Blake, and she's as well known for spiritual renditions on the organ as Reverend Buddy Dee is famous for Saving souls."

"Mama said that after supper, we'd all come over to the Revival tonight," I said. "You and me and Mama and Papa."

"That'll be nice."

"Do folks really get Saved?"

"They really do, Babe. They really do."

"Honest?"

"Honest to Peter. Tent shows may be backwoodsy to some city people I know, but every church has a mission, Babe. A purpose, so please remember that."

"I'll remember."

"Traveling churches can sometimes reach down into the gutter and lift a man or a woman up, and before you know, they're on their feet and standing in the light."

"The way you say it," I said, "it sounds good."

"Hope to goodness."

"What's it like, getting Saved?"

"Well," said Aunt Hobart as she tapped her Red Cross shoe in time with "Golden Garden," "I'd have to say that getting Saved is a little bit like getting scrubbed in a good hot bath."

"A *bath?*"

"Hush now. A bath isn't so cussed. Wager we'll both need one before supper. But like I was saying, getting Saved is rather like being born for a second time."

"Does it make ya clean?"

Aunt Hobart smiled down at me. Like my father and mother, she owned a very good face for smiling. "Yes," she said, "very clean. It makes your soul feel fresher than new snow on a Christmas morn."

"Does it last?"

"Well," laughed Aunt Hobart, "that's exactly why Saving is a wee bit like a bath."

"Why?"

"Because a bath doesn't last forever. And yet, Babe, we all do need one once in a while."

Something in the way she said it answered my next question. I was about to ask my aunt if she'd ever got herself Saved. I sort of figured she did, because Aunt Hobart was the kind of person that nobody'd throw away. A man appeared with a sign which he was waving around in such a fussy manner that it was hard to read. But finally he settled down and I made out the letters:

SATAN PLAYS BASEBALL ON SUNDAY

"Is that true?" I asked Aunt Hobart.

"Some folks may think so."

"They can't say things like that," I said, wanting to grab the dumb old sign, tear it down, and rip it up to bits.

"Oh," said Aunt Hobart, "*yes* they can."

"They can?"

"Truly," she said, "and they have as much privilege to oppose baseball as you do to play it. That's what America is all about. I have the same right to be a Baptist as . . . who was that large giant of a gentleman who tripped as he was bundling the umpire?"

"Oh," I said, "that's Uncle Albert. He belongs to Angelo."

"I see . . . then as Uncle Albert has the right to be proud of Italy. Make any sense?"

"Some. Will there be a fight?"

"Perhaps, but let's do our darnedest to shortstop it. Lots of folks, Babe, get their summer blood a bit too heated up."

"Over what?"

"Well, over baseball and over Bibles."

Everything that Aunt Hobart ever said to me always sounded clean and friendly (except for tagging a runner on first). So I guess that's how I figured out that Aunt Hobart really had been Saved.

"Come on," she said, "I got me an idea."

It was then that I heard her pleasantly telling one of the men in black clothes that if the JEHOVAH people could *please* move their wagons back a mite, to the right of that white line for an hour, she would attend the Revival tonight and bring all her kinfolk. And, she added, she was planning on a sizable donation for the collection plate.

It worked! They moved their black wagons before they unhitched. And it made me ponder if Aunt Hobart also knew about politics and poker.

As we walked over toward the pitcher's mound, I could still hear the organ playing "There's a Golden Garden in the Bye and Bye" and the old hymn seemed to be making a very sweet promise, about the Hereafter and all.

"Aunt Hobart, could McGinty ever get Saved?"

She nodded. "Indeed he could."

"And could the Reverend Buddy Dee do it?"

"If he can't," she said, "perhaps someone else could, yet in a different way. You see, Babe, getting Saved is really based on love, and believing. And if anything will rescue Dan, it will be someone who believes in him with all her heart."

I knew she meant *me*.

CHAPTER 12

"It's a sprain."

"You sure, Doc?"

"Of course I'm sure," snapped Doc Tussy. "Don't you think I know a thing or two about medicine and can size up a sprained ankle when I see one?"

No one answered.

Crowded around the pitcher's mound there must have been near to two hundred people, and we were all looking down at the way Doc Tussy's hands had pulled up the dusty black pantsleg to examine Albert Morelli's rapidly swelling extremity. Doc gave the ankle a sudden professional tweak, as though to let folks know that he was on the case, causing his patient to yelp in pain.

"Yyyaaahhh!" howled Uncle Albert, who then glowered at Doc and launched into a long string of Italian phrases that seemed to be other than medical terms. Murph then had more things to say to Uncle Albert; again, not in medical terms, which caused the drum major of the Sons of Italy band to cry.

Aunt Hobart was on the scene and she used her own white hanky to blot the sorrow from Uncle Albert's big face. Looking at what was pinned to his shirt, I identified a Dick Tracy decoder. I concluded that Uncle Albert also listened to the radio at five o'clock on weekday afternoons and, like me, mailed away his boxtops from Quaker Puffed Rice.

"Play ball!" said Murph.

Doc Tussy held up his hands. "Wait! This man can't be moved."

"Can't be moved? He's on the pitcher's mound," yelled Murph.

"Don't matter," said Doc Tussy, obviously enjoying his moment in the center of things as he took command. "He's got a sprain and stays put until relief gets here."

"What relief?"

"Just a figure of speech," said Doc. "Now, as I was just about to say—"

"Look," said Murph, pointing a finger into Doc Tussy's chest, "you ain't running this here game."

"Then who is?" snapped Doc.

"I am," Murph said.

"You? Don't make me laugh. This *happens* to be an emergency, and so if there's a doctor present, *he* takes over."

"Good," said Murph. "Lucky for us there ain't no doctor present."

"I don't have to stand here and take this." Doc's eye had his *just wait until you get my bill* look.

"No," said Murph, "you can go back to your seat like everybody else in Durkee's Lot and shut your mouth."

"Are you telling *me* to shut up?" hollered Doc.

"Shut up, Doc," somebody said, "and lend us a hand."

We got Albert up into the bin of the pickup truck that Lick Donovan had backed over to near where Italy's Son rolled around in the dust. When his Dick Tracy decoder fell off into the sand, I saw McGinty pick it up and pin it back on Uncle Albert's sweaty shirt.

"Can ya beat that?" asked an irate Murph. "That clumsy noodle falls on me, and he gets *himself* busted up. Serves him right."

Even though Murph was yelling "Play ball," we all stood around the pitcher's mound giving Albert Morelli advice on how to care for a sprained ankle. Up in the pickup truck, Doc Tussy was still yelling instructions to anyone who would listen. No one listened. We all had to hunt for the baseball and when it was located, a Warrior ran over and tagged Dan McGinty, claiming that Murph had never called time.

Needless to add, Murph ruled that he *had* called time out, and McGinty was restored to second base.

Gil Haskin singled.

In left, I saw Dilworth come up with the ball and McGinty tag third and chug for home. It was a shock to see how fast Dan could move. Rounding third base, his cleats just nipped the inside corner of the bag as his body banked, arms pumping the air, legs driving inside one work sock and one purple stocking. But Dan wasn't going to make it. He'd be out a mile. Luckily, the peg from left was wide, about a yard and a half. But then Gus Gitbo made a good catch, mask flung off, and was ready with the tag.

McGinty slid home.

On his hip, cleats high and churning, I saw Sober cut into Gus Gitbo. Murph had the call ready. His arm was even on the way up, as there wasn't a soul in Durkee's Lot, possibly including Butler, who couldn't see that Gus put the nip on Sober.

"Out!" yelled Murph, against his will, dashing even his own principles of foul play into the dust along with their catcher and our pitcher. But as Murph yelled "Out!" Gus Gitbo dropped the ball. I could see that tagging a runner who slides in with spikes up and kicking was no easy task.

"Safe!" hollered a happy Murph, spreading his arms.

Dan McGinty slowly got up on his feet. The Canby crowd enjoyed a full minute of deafening insanity: horns blowing, people yelling his name, hats in the air. Hawg dropped his hot dog. There was a bloody nick on Gus Gitbo's hand, and Sober sort of looked like he said he was sorry, which didn't seem to smooth the relationship any. Gus said something to

Dan, which I couldn't hear as the Sons of Italy attacked another rendition. As Sober McGinty came to our dugout, we all got up on our feet to hug him and punch him and tell him it was one heck of a mean slide. Dan sat down next to me, breathing as loud as the crowd.

"What did Gus say to you?" I asked him.

"Said he'd a' done the same thing to me."

"He sure would," I agreed.

"It's part of the game. But if you want to know the straight of it, Babe, I really am sorry I spiked Gus. I've knowed Gus Gitbo for twenty years. More than that. I feel like a rat. And if I had it to do over, I'd a' come home with a clean slide."

"Honest?"

"Yup. I don't know what made me do it, Babe. Maybe I just wanted to show people that I was still Dan McGinty instead of a smelly sack of old clothes."

"About your slide . . ."

"What about it?"

"Was it cheating, Dan?"

He spat out a yellow jet of tobacco juice, continuing to chew. There was still dust on the side of his shoulder, and my hand returned some of it to Durkee's Lot as I brushed him off.

"Cheating? Maybe yes and maybe no."

"*You* wouldn't cheat, Dan."

"I play to win. Babe, if I'd a slid into home

headfirst, making a belly dive and reaching for the plate with my hand, Gus would a' done something."

"Like what?"

"He'd stomped his iron across my fingers or stuffed the ball down my throat."

"Honest?"

McGinty's hand pulled up the knee of his striped knickers and there was a lump on his calf, red and swollen. "See that, Babe?"

"Wow!"

"Gus put the tag on me a little harder than he had to. Just so I'd remember him, come Monday."

"Is he mean?"

"Gus? Heck no, he ain't mean. Me and Gus logged together one winter, up north of here. He's a good worker and he always done his share."

"Well, he sort of looks mean," I said.

"It's the mask."

"Will Farnum doesn't."

Dan smiled. "That's because you see Will here in the dugout with his mask off and his nature smiling. You should see Will from out on the mound."

"What's he look like from out there?"

"When he hunkers down over that plate, behind all the paraphernalia he wears, I feel like I'm fixed to chuck the ball at some soldier from Saturn."

There were no more hits for us. At least, not that inning. Nor the next. I didn't have too many chores to mind, except to make three more trips to Riley

Shattuck's establishment and to fetch a Grape Crush and a dog for Hawg Hogarth.

The Catfish were in the field, which left the dugout empty except for Hawg and me and Jake Broda, who finally arrived in uniform. Jake was a good guy, but he never came around on time. Not even to practice. Maybe that was the reason Hawg always started Luke Fish at short instead of Jake, and Vernal at second.

"How's his arm?" Jake asked nobody, looking out at the mound at McGinty.

"Well," said Hawg, "it's still hangin' down from his shoulder."

We got out of the inning. The score was still 3–2 in Wiggin's favor, but at least we were coming in to bat. From somewhere (off the field, thank goodness), the Sons of Italy battled with Verdi, as earlier, the Canby Silver-Cornet Band had contested the arrangements of John Philip Sousa. In school, Mr. Harley Romano told us that Verdi was his favorite composer, but it was apparent that he had done little to defend the works of Mr. Verdi from the Sons of Italy, their brasses, and their drums.

I had always wondered why Harley Romano directed the Silver-Cornets and not the Italian-American instrumentalists. So I asked him in school. He said that he could not listen to the Sons of Italy as he loved Verdi too much.

Again I tried to get McGinty to put some food in

his stomach. He just wouldn't eat. As I was returning from the hot-dog stand, to help prevent Hawg Hogarth from reading Empty, I saw Lick Donovan take back a brown paper bag from Dan. And when I sat next to McGinty, his breath burned with whiskey. I couldn't talk. It was as if my throat was choked up. I wanted to turn around and punch Lick Donovan. His eyes were about as red as Dan's. This, I told myself, was a sorry way to celebrate Sunday.

One more whiff of Sober McGinty and I darn near left his side to sit with Aunt Hobart. But I didn't.

"You hungry, Dan?" I asked him.

"Nope. Just thirsty."

Smiling at me, he got up and helped himself to a dipper of cold water. As the blue-speckled bowl of the dipper came up and over his face as he drained it dry, his eye winked my way. And I winked back at McGinty.

In the last of the eighth, Wiggin was still leading us 3–2. Of our two runs, McGinty had singled in the first and slid home for the second.

Cecil Snow flied out to center. And then Will Farnum struck out. Two out and nobody on, and Dan McGinty carried his yellow bat to the plate. The Canby crowd loved Dan *if* the Catfish were winning. But we were losing today, and so the rumble of the fans was less than enthusiastic.

Ball one. Sherman Gitbo's fast ball took off and Gus had to hop out of his crouch to haul it in.

Behind the plate, I could see Gus Gitbo was hot and
tiring. When there was no Canby runner on base,
he'd sink down on his right knee to receive Sherm's
pitch.

Ball two.

"That's the eye, McGinty!"

When I heard Hawg cough, I figured he was
horning out a take sign to Sober, and sure enough
. . . the 2–0 delivery came in, and Dan just watched
it breeze by for a strike. Too bad, as it was a fat
pitch. McGinty could have parked it.

Strike two.

Dan swung on a bad ball, missed, and 'twisted
down in the dust. People laughed, as he looked a lot
drunker than he was. Ball three, a full count. The
next pitch was inside, with as much on it as Sherman
Gitbo could put. I saw Dan try to loosen his cleats
and jump out of the way, just before the ball buried
in his stomach. Again McGinty went down.

And stayed down.

CHAPTER 13

Everybody just groaned.

As I ran toward the plate where Dan McGinty lay on the ground, Murph and Gus were bending over him. McGinty was curled up on his side, knees up, hands holding his gut. On his face I read the pain, as though his hurt was painted on his cheeks in red letters.

In from the mound ran Sherman Gitbo, and I wanted to pick up the ball and throw it at him with all my might. Until I saw his face, also in pain.

"Sober," said Sherman, "I'm real sorry. Ya know I didn't mean . . ." Down on one knee, Sherman touched Dan's shoulder, lifted his head off the dirt, making a pillow with his glove.

"You okay, Dan?" asked Murph.

"Give him a drink!" somebody yelled, and there was laughter that followed. Hearing it made my fists double up.

"He ain't hurt," hollered some other voice. "He's just empty."

"Can you sit up, Dan?" I asked him.

Opening his eyes, he looked at me, and sort of threw me half a grin. Yet his hands still held his stomach. We got him up on his knees, then up on his feet, with one of his arms yoking Hawg's beefy shoulder, and another around Gus Gitbo. All action stopped as he limped toward our dugout.

"Wait," said Dan.

"What's the matter?" asked Hawg, as he and Gus and Dan stood still, halfway from home plate to our bench.

"I'm up to bat," said Dan.

"Hell you are," snorted Hawg.

"Gimme a drink."

"A *drink?*"

"Yeah, ask Lick. Hey Lick! C'mere, will ya?"

Already there was a crowd around Dan, and Lick Donovan (his bottle in his bag) added one more. McGinty helped himself to a long pull, went back into the hitter's box, picked up his bat . . . and struck the air as if he still wanted to hit. Like he didn't even know that Murph was for sure going to award him a base.

McGinty limped down to first.

Gil Haskin singled to left, a solid one-hopper to Bert Dilworth's glove. Canby cheered, and then hollered in rage at McGinty who had not left first.

Bert's peg to second was perfect and Dan was

forced out on what could have been runners on first and second, and Luke Fish and Harwood Mix to follow. That is if Luke got a hit. Top of the order, our main chance, and we all saw Dan blow it away. I figured Hawg would get sore, but he didn't.

"McGinty is hurting," Hawg told me.

"Can he go another inning?"

"He's gotta. It's our only chance."

Then it struck me. I saw Jake Broda out in center field instead of Larry O'Toole.

"Hey! Where's Larry?"

"He went home. His old lady is down with grippe and it's close to chore time. Jake'll play. Center ain't our main worry. Ya know, all of a sudden I ain't a bit hungry."

Up to bat, facing Dan, was Hank Gitbo who singled the first pitch like he knew what was coming. Jerry Keen hit back to the box, with double play written all over its one bounce. Then the ball skipped out of Dan's glove (my glove) and rolled toward short. No play on either runner; and now the Warriors had two on and nobody out. Both on account of Dan McGinty.

"Take the bum out," a man yelled. "He's a pink elephant."

Even though their best hitter, Jack Gitbo, was now at the plate with a big bat, I figured old Injun Joe would not have Jack swing away and hit a double-play ball to our infield.

"Watch the bunt!" I yelled, hands cupping my mouth and hoping Dan would hear.

Ball one. Ball two. Ball three. And the Canby crowd was no longer with Dan, as though they actually thought our pitcher was on Wiggin's side.

Strike one.

But the next pitch was perfect for a bunt, which Jack Gitbo dropped about twenty feet in front of the plate. Both runners broke, for second and for third. But our catcher was up and to the ball, ready to throw to third for the front runner. And then Dan lurched forward off the mound, trying to field the ball, seeing Will Farnum's quick reaction, and then stumbling to his right so Will could make the throw to first. Trouble was, Will was throwing to third, and all McGinty did was block the play.

Bases loaded, and all three runners safe.

"You're all washed up, Sober! Or washed down."

"Turn in your suit, ya has-been!"

"Heat gotcha, McGinty? Or is it the firewater?"

Boos were coming from all directions now, not just from the excited Wiggin crowd. Even with my fingers stuck in my ears, as I sat beside Hawg in our dugout, I could hear the hollering from Canby fans. Why did they suddenly hate Dan McGinty so much? Was beating Wiggin so important? Heck it was.

"He's all through," said Hawg.

"No he isn't."

"Yeah. Our old boy's having his last Sunday. And

I'm like you, kid. I can't bear to look. You should a' seen McGinty twenty years ago. Or away back before that when we was all in school. Boy, he could whip in a strike from center field."

"You're done, McGinty!" someone yelled.

"Hang up your glove, Sober!"

"Go hang *yourself!*"

Sober stood in a daze out on the mound, as if the ball was too heavy to hold. He looked over at the bench.

Until I glanced at Hawg and saw a tear running down his big ruddy face, I figured that maybe I wasn't going to cry too much. And then Hawg's big arm went around me so my face could bury against his shaking shoulder. Together we wept, the two of us alone in the dugout. My entire body was trembling, and I just couldn't watch the game any more. Not that the score mattered. It didn't. And I never wanted to see another baseball game, or be mascot for the Canby Catfish. Not after today.

"What's . . . he . . . doing?" I managed to ask Hawg, even though my voice was so choked up that the words could sob out only one at a time.

"Dan's pitchin' his last game." Hawg's chin trembled.

It was the first time I'd heard Hawg ever call McGinty by his real name. Hawg's voice wasn't deep, as usual, and what he said was as quiet as a prayer. And every bit as respectful.

"Ya know, Babe, it ain't like it's even July," said Hawg. "It's sorta like November, and we're watching a leaf turn brown. And fall."

"We . . . better . . . do something for him," I said.

"Nothin'. Ain't nothin' we can do, and believe me when I tell ya, we all tried."

The hot afternoon sun was screaming down on the flat diamond of Durkee's Lot, where every eye watched a man with a hurting belly (and a seven on his back) stretch down and grab some sand to dry off his fingers. He didn't toe the rubber. All he did was look around as if he was lost, or confused, as though he didn't even know that this was his hometown, and his friends had all come to Durkee's Lot to see him play.

"Dan," I said softly.

Oscar Sanchez was the hitter, and Wiggin was yelling for Sober McGinty to pitch to him. Nobody out, and bases loaded. But no ball was thrown. People booed and hissed, yet causing no response from the mound, where Sober took off his cap and wiped his brow with the right sleeve of his purple underjersey. He was reeling.

Bit by bit, the crowd quieted down, as though expecting McGinty to come up with an uncommon delivery, or an outstanding play, as he had so often. Suddenly, it was quiet, as though no one dared to move or breathe. It was as if we could hear the July heat beating in our ears.

Then, looking at the white baseball in his hand, McGinty slowly raised it to his mouth and gently kissed it.

No one spoke.

Slowly, he turned and stumbled down off the mound, weaving in our direction until he made it to our dugout; where, as our big manager got to his feet, he collapsed in Hawg's arms. McGinty's uniform was dark with sweat. Hawg lifted him up as Dan's purple cap fell off and into the dust. Never before had I noticed how thin McGinty had become. In Hawg's massive arms, he looked brittle and pale and childlike.

"I gotcha, Dan," said Hawg.

We eased him down onto the bench. But then McGinty was shaking his head, as if to tell us he didn't want to lie on the long wooden seat inside the dugout.

"Outside," panted Dan. "In the sunshine, where I can look at the sky."

We carried him outside.

"Ya know," said McGinty, "I want to feel the grass on my face." He was lying on his back, eyes half closed, mouth open, and breathing heavily, as though just lying there was too much for him.

"I'll fetch Doc," said Hawg.

"No," Dan shook his head. "Get a preacher."

"Which one?"

Dan smiled. "Does it matter?"

People were standing nearby, motionless, some in baseball uniforms and some not, yet all keeping a respectful distance away. Hawg dashed off about as fast as a man of his tonnage could hustle. Alone on my knees, I held Dan McGinty's face in my hands. My eyes were wet, and I couldn't quite see, but I felt he was looking up at me.

"Babe," he said. His voice was afar off.

"I'm . . . right beside you, Dan."

"Here." He handed me the ball that had been jammed in the webbing of my glove. "Grip it, Babe."

I held the ball as he'd so often showed me. "Like this?"

"Yeah. Open your fork, so's your fingers ride the seams."

"I will, Dan."

"Hold it, Babe. Real tight."

"I promise."

"Don't never let go."

"I won't ever," I told him.

"Keep that ball. Keep it like we won."

I nodded my head, squeezing the baseball inside my fist as if I could help Dan McGinty hold on to everything that was now slipping away.

"Babe?"

"Here I am, Dan. Right here."

He blinked. "Did the sun go down?"

"A bit. Getting on late."

"Cows'll be coming home," said Dan.

I nodded. Never had I thought of early sundown as a sad time of day, yet suddenly it was; as though the light was fading the sky, washing away the blue, and then to replace it with gray, and black. Everyone was silent. My arms hugged his neck, and against my face, I felt the raw gray stubble of his whiskers. I wanted to say thank you to Dan McGinty for letting all of us in Canby be a part of his life.

"Good game, Dan."

He never answered. As his tired lungs worked in and out, I closed my eyes to inhale part of his breathing. Holding his last breath inside me until it was sweet again.

ROBERT NEWTON PECK comes from a long line of Vermont farmers. At the age of seventeen, during World War II, he joined the 88th Infantry Division and after the war returned home to attend Rollins College. Although a prolific writer, author of the enormously popular A DAY NO PIGS WOULD DIE, Mr. Peck has not limited himself to purely literary pursuits. He is an enthusiastic public speaker, has killed hogs, worked in a paper mill, and made his living as a lumberjack. In his spare time he enjoys playing ragtime piano and the old Scottish game of curling.